About the editors:

Alison Campbell is from Aberdeen and presently lives in North London. She is co-editor of *The Man Who Loved Presents* (The Women's Press, 1991) and co-author of *Are You Asleep, Rabbit?*, a children's picture book (HarperCollins, 1990).

Caroline Hallett lives and works in North London, where she has helped to set up a counselling service for young people. Writing is an interest that persists alongside job, training and family of three small children. She writes short stories and is gradually adding to a number which she hopes to make into a collection.

Jenny Palmer was born in Lancashire and educated at Reading University. She is a world traveller, now settled in Hackney. She teaches English at Goldsmith's and King's Colleges to speakers of other languages and has published widely on Third World Issues in *Spare Rib, Outwrite, The Socialist* and *Everywoman*. She is now completing her second novel arising out of a recent trip to Bolivia, together with a collection of short stories.

Marijke Woolsey lives in South Tottenham in North London with her husband and two daughters. She writes short stories and novels. As well as co-editing *The Man Who Loved Presents* and finishing the rewrites of her third novel, *The Eye of the Beholder*, she is currently editing a collection of women's short stories on the theme of horror.

Also by Alison Campbell, Caroline Hallett, Jenny Palmer and Marijke Woolsey from The Women's Press:

The Man Who Loved Presents: Seasonal Stories (1991)

The
Plot Against
Mary

more seasonal stories

**EDITED BY ALISON CAMPBELL,
CAROLINE HALLETT, JENNY PALMER
AND MARIJKE WOOLSEY**

First published by The Women's Press Limited 1992
A member of the Namara Group
34 Great Sutton Street, London EC1V 0DX

British Library Cataloguing in Publication Data
Plot Against Mary: More Seasonal Stories
  I. Campbell, Alison
  808.83 [FS]

ISBN 0 7043 4328 2

Typeset by Falcon Typographic Art Ltd, Fife, Scotland
Printed and bound in Great Britain by
BPCC Hazells Ltd.
Member of BPCC Ltd.

Contents

Foreword

In 1991 we edited an anthology of women's seasonal stories entitled *The Man Who Loved Presents*. We were so excited by its success that when The Women's Press suggested a second anthology, we felt we wanted to take on the challenge. We wondered if there was enough material out there to warrant a follow-up. We needn't have worried; the stories flowed in. The theme seemed to strike a chord with women, and we were inundated with a host of angels, a deluge of deaths and births, biblical reworkings and almost no cold turkey!

Once again our homes were buzzing with editorial meetings, and we sifted and selected to meet our three-month deadline. We are pleased to present a second feast of delectable tales from both established and unpublished women writers. We feel we have made a strong, humorous and often poignant collection where women triumph, sometimes in the least promising circumstances. We hope the book will surprise and delight our readers as much as it did us.

Thanks to our editor, Kathy Gale, at The Women's Press and to everyone who has supported and encouraged us.

Alison Campbell
Caroline Hallett
Jenny Palmer
Marijke Woolsey

The Strongwoman

Glyn Brown

'I think not, Gabriel,' said Mary with a smile. 'I had my heart set on women's wrestling.'

She continued to sit at the table, quite still apart from the rhythmic flexing of her arm, holding a sand-filled bag of muslin which was acting as a primitive dumbbell. The air was limpid, warm for the time of day – early morning – but not unpleasant, and the sky was of a wholly pleasing pinkish blue, the way it is ideally supposed to be at six or so. It was one of the most appetising mornings Mary had known, and not just because of this in its way flattering meeting and project proposal. Today, she was completing every exercise she set herself without strain. Mary was dedicated to her pursuit of fitness, but not unhealthily so. She had begun getting up earlier than usual some months back so that she could do a little preparatory limbering before she milked the goats; she was pretty strong now, as the goats could testify.

Gabriel shifted to rest the major part of his weight on his right foot. He was right-handed and he preferred at all times to work from the right side of his body, particularly when things were cutting up a little rough and he foresaw the need to think clearly and quickly and round, so to speak, the wayward sheep off at the pass. He cleared his golden throat. 'You do not feel, O holiest one, that it's time to put away the toys of impressionable youth and do the right thing by your man –'

At this, Mary's chin lifted smartly, and an eyebrow with it. She had very black eyebrows for a mousy-haired dame.

'– and by all of us upon the planet, most blessed among women?' There was a testy silence. 'Well?'

Mary, sweating lightly, transferred the muslin bag to her other hand – the left and strongest – and, resting her elbow on the table, began to pump the weight in sprightly repetitions. Gabriel, waiting anxiously, noticed her head was bobbing gently in time. She was counting instead of thinking about his record-breaking suggestion. With an effort, he roped down his temper and wheedled sycophantically, 'Mary, holy queen, have you considered the Lord our Father's generous offer?'

'. . . three, four, five and six. I don't believe this, give it a rest!'

A couple of strands of Mary's hair were wet now and stuck to her face. As far as Gabriel could tell, she was still counting, but under her breath. It had to be said, her deltoids looked huge, they really did. Toned and very muscular. For a woman.

'Sitting dumbbell curls aren't the . . . uh, *uh* . . . easiest things in the world to do when you're . . . huh, uh . . . talking.' She stopped, held her shoulder and revolved it in a circle, then picked up another weight from the sandy floor and began to do the exercise with alternating arms.

Gabriel felt something of a fool. 'I can see you're busy.'

'Oh, you can see that, can you?' grunted the virgin. Veins stood out on her chest and on her pale inner arms between the curvaceous triceps and biceps.

Gabriel bit his very full, not to say cherubic, lip. What was she going to look like if this sort of business went on? What would happen if they pulled it off and even Mary believed she was going to shell the Son of God, like a celestial peapod? None of your religious artists were going to have the paint to render arms that size in their true, hideous dimensions – although there was, if he were honest, something strangely sexy about those muscles. But 'sexy' wouldn't help them. Everything was going grotesquely wrong. He touched his temple. Hell, it was warm today. Another scorcher lining up.

'Dearly beloved, I depart from thee now. But rest assured that I will pay thee future visits, and soon. Think, I strongly beseech, on what I have said.'

'That's three sets of fifteen reps!' panted Mary, sweat soaking the back of her simple shift. 'Oh, sorry, Gabriel. Will do.'

'So?'
'It may be a longer job than we thought.'
Joseph of the house of David put his face in his hands. That was often where he felt it should be, of late. Oh, it wasn't a bad face, it wasn't jowly or mean-mouthed. Joseph spared the onlooker crossed eyes, flapping, sticky-out ears and warts. It was just a boring face. Unexciting. A visage, any-way, that didn't turn on his consort. From between clammy fingers, his voice leaked across the table. 'Why longer?'

'Because she has other things to do, bub.' Gabriel took the edge of the blond moustache he'd made out of goat hairs and attached to his upper lip with candle wax, and snapped it smartly away. Tenderly, he rubbed his reddened skin.

'Things? What *things*?' Joseph might be Gabriel's best buddy but boy, could he be difficult. 'She's a girl, right? She's my wife! The "things" she does are get up at six, get my grub, milk the goats, sort out my packed lunch, clean the house, go shopping for my dinner, have a natter with Elisabeth or Rachel or my mum – *if* she's got time – cook me something tasty for when I get back and then' – his stubby digits kneaded the wooden table's edge – 'get in my bed and fuck me stupid. Not necessarily always in that order.'

'I'm not sure she sees it quite that way. But she'll come round eventually.' Gabriel dusted off his palms and, picking up a rusty fork, rounded on his dish of mutton stew. Lamb for the fourth time in a week. Sheep and goats, goats and sheep, it seemed to be all his life consisted of. Although, certainly, he was seeing a fair amount of Mary. Always, unfortunately, in heavy disguise.

'Oh, she will? How about the tiny fact that my beloved declares she'll never grace my bed, that she finds me as attractive as a millepede and, quite apart from this, she (the most desirable woman for hundreds of thousands of miles) is dedicated to her art of wrestling and will put that first at all times?'

Joseph looked rabid, frantic. His dry lips quivered. Gabriel had to admit it, his friend was not the most magnetic of libidinal prospects. He glanced away, recalling Mary's rounded, fawn arms moving silently in the dawn light. Something grated painfully on his ear. Damn, was that 'Smoke Gets in Your Eyes' again? In a country where every fire belched fumes, couldn't one single inn provide a lyre player with an original tune? He swung tetchily back to his hirsute crony.

'No one believes that baloney, Mac. Be realistic. It's what girls *say*.' Gabe cleared his lying throat. 'In any case, she's a wild one. Bit of a tearaway. You knew that before the betrothal.'

'Yup. I'd heard it.' Joseph spooned up his own stew. Rancid gravy dribbled down his chin and sloppy chews deformed his speech. 'I just thought it meant she'd be crazy in the sack.'

Gabriel leaned bulkily across the bench. 'See here, hombre, if she'd been that way inclined since you two jumped the broomstick, we all know Joseph aka Mouth-Bigger-Than-Mount-Tabor would've told the whole of Nazareth, no? Where would our scheme be then? We'd both be condemned to a lifetime of exhausting manual labour, me chasing flocks of sheep hither and yon, over hill and dale, day in and day out, and you for ever a lowly carpenter.'

'Not as lowly as a shepherd.'

There was a momentary lull in the boisterous male chatter around the two compadres, in which the racket of a whining lyre could be heard. 'Smoke Gets in Your Eyes' ended on a poignant rising falsetto, and the soothing lullaby of 'Sheep May Safely Graze' commenced. Gabriel smacked his forehead with a clenched fist. 'But as it *is*,' he went on, 'we all know you haven't had it. Boy, do we know. So when one fine day Mary – who repeatedly claims she wouldn't skip the light ahem fantastic with you even with a sack upon your bonce (or, to be fair, anyone else, and that girl packs quite a punch) – when she tells the world she's been visited by the Holy Ghost and is about to bear the Saviour which is Christ the Lord, who's going to doubt it?'

'Er . . .'

'No one'll doubt it. And who'll get the glory?'

'Ah . . .'

'You will, wacker.'

'Any woman can have a baby, I guess.'

'You're darn tootin'. But it's the husband takes the credit for what comes out. Mary – well, we see her as a vessel, a receptacle used by God, belonging to you.'

Joseph was staring intently at a strip of loose skin adjacent to his thumbnail. Gabriel's hands were artful birds, describing scenarios of future bliss in so many multi-navigational arcs and trajectories.

'Ah yes, indeed, it's so clear. Mary, believing she's the transporter of a very special bundle of joy, at once becomes selflessly maternal, casting aside her errant weightlifting ways and admitting gladly to the role she was born for: no more but very certainly no less than, say, a pot boiling on a stove, bubbling with its precious *plat du jour*, a casserole, a skillet, a veritable cauldron, to all intents and purposes. She simmers and she steams with heat' (Gabriel smacked lewd and labial chops) 'but, when the dish is done, it's Joseph – if not the chef then undoubtedly the *maître d'* – who blushingly' (he flutters full lashes) 'claims responsibility and justly receives praise. Fame. Oh, huge amounts of it, endless fame! And such riches showered upon you, you'll need to employ your trusty pal Gabe as accountant and general money-manager. Am I right or am I . . .'

'Right, right, you're right.' Joseph's tongue slipped lasciviously around a piece of slimy gristle. Mary, Mary – she was *bloody* contrary but it was true, the scheme must work; hadn't it been his own idea in the first place, which Gabriel had so effortlessly perfected? And once Mary had conceived, she'd be flooded with the hormones she now so patently lacked (he'd observed it a million times in the newly pregnant) and she'd be randy as a goat. If he and his trusty henchman could just get the deed done, two plump birds – Mary and money – would fall into their laps with one stone. It was too inspired not to come off.

'I don't think you quite understand, Gabriel or whatever your name is.' Mary was rapidly hauling a pail of water from the bottom of a very deep well. 'If I don't keep these muscles toned they go loose, give way and turn to flab. Now, if I'm pregnant, how long do you think anyone's going to let me carry on working out? And by anyone, I principally mean Joseph who, despite his bluff big-talk and masculine braggadocio, is a superstitious and worrisome cove. (Something I found endearing for five light-headed minutes and what did it get me? Engaged.) Any old wives' tale and he believes it, so once I'm up the stick it'll be the devil's own job to . . .'

'Hush, breathe not that word, the name of the tempter.' Gabriel was considering Mary's soft pink lips. He realised he'd lost his train of thought for today. 'I behold that you are not open to reasonable discussion this morning, Mary of Nazareth. I shall return on the morrow, but consider – only allow the Holy Spirit to visit thee and all Galilee shall call thy offspring blessed.'

Mary, hand on a hip, gave him an appraising glance. 'You know, Gabriel,' she observed, 'you're a little on the solid side for an angel but you're really not a bad-looking guy.' And then she winked playfully. Gabriel swallowed hard.

'I see there must needs be many meetings between us, my child, for verily thou shalt be convinced of my truth.' Flustered and breathless, he turned and thundered heavily away over the bluff, flapping his arms with a certain ungainly agitation.

Mary turned back to the well, chuckling. 'Nitwits,' she said to no one in particular.

'Let's give up. The thing's a joke and a sham. I drove a nail into my thumb this morning. A plank of sapele smacked me in the eye about four o'clock and all I was doing was planing it. I've got constant gutache from nervous tension. Also, I quite like the look of that girl Hepzibah . . .'

'Superstitious and worrisome, she wasn't kidding.'

'Say what?'

'Not a thing. Thinking about m'dinner.'

'I don't know why we're going on with it, you and I, two men, strong men, handsome men many would think. I myself could have any damned woman I wanted, is that true or isn't it? Yet you feel we should see this through?'

Gabriel picked at a thread of lamb stuck between his teeth. He said, 'Mary's thighs, shapely as sin as, skirts rucked and tucked into her waistband, she scrubs the stone floors of your simple dwelling.'

He said, 'Mary's deep and brown cleavage, displayed as she pounds clean the washing on flat stones fringeing the stream.'

He said, 'Mary's waist, slim and supple as honey as she hangs that washing up to dry. The way Mary turns her head from your apparently repulsive kisses, the haughty fragility of her long cheekbones, gazelle-like, and her rosy earlobes, just right for nibbling.'

'We see it through,' replied Joseph, tipping a jug of water over his feverish head. 'Now, what's the plan for disguising me as the Holy Ghost?'

Gabriel looked at the wall. There was a sudden truculent set to his jaw.

'Two sets of ten standing dumbbell flyes, one set each of alternating dumbbell kickbacks, twenty leg lunges, hundreds of toe raises – because you can do those anywhere, in the house, in the market, while you're talking to a friend – and I'm up to fifty situps a day. By attaching cannily improvised weights to a sturdy branch, I've made myself a barbell. Up to three sets of twelve reps with the barbell press behind the neck, and five sets of six wrist curls. Three times fifteen squats with the barbell, for the gluteus maximus. Now I can run faster than any man in Nazareth. I've proved it.'

'I expect you have. I'm sure you have. You're a very attractive girl.'

'I'm a woman.'

'Don't correct your mother, dear.'

'Sorry, Ma.'

'And I know you're a woman. As such, what do you intend to do with all these muscles, if I might be so bold? They'd probably serve you well in the, excuse me, marriage bed. Fine strong pelvic floor, I imagine you possess. You know what that's good for.'

'Do I?'

'Coyness doesn't suit you, Mary. Knit one, purl one, rib rib rib. There, that should fit your father's head. On second thoughts, can you reach me that final ball of wool?'

'The red?' Mary began to unwind the spun fleece. 'I know what you're driving at, but the thing is, Joseph's a puny wimp and I'm not. And I've found out he isn't very bright either. You'll never believe it, but he and his pal have cooked up this plot to convince me I'm going to be bedded by an archangel and bear the Son of God. Imagine being fucked –'

'*Language . . .*'

'Sorry, by an angel. Like suffocating inside a pillow. Like being mauled by a chick. No, what I'm after is something to really pit myself against. Think there're any lady wrestlers in Galilee at all? Or, if not, what about Samaria?'

'What's new?'

'You heard about the river scene, I take it?'

'No. I've stopped listening to gossip. Since lately it's always about her.'

'Hm, yes, and it was again. In an excess of energy, she apparently took over the pounding and pummelling of an elderly woman's washing at the pool where they all cluster, regular as clockwork, at the top of the sudsy stream. This aged bat had raddled arms, veiny, useless; couldn't bash the vestments the way they gotta be bashed to clean 'em up. So Mary did it.'

Joseph took the tip of a lock of hair and appeared to be examining it for split ends. Then he gripped the fatty upper part of his arm and squeezed. There was muscle, but not much. Comparatively. 'And?'

'And then she did everyone else's. Trilling away all the time, singing like a lark.'

Joseph grunted. 'And here I was, thinking it might calm her down a bit if she imagined she was doing something worthwhile and philanthropic, like bearing the Messiah.'

'*Au contraire*, the philanthropic seems to excite her. It gives her energy, wearing amounts.'

Joseph picked at a spot. 'She loves the razzmatazz, though.'

'A sucker for it. As she took her blushing bow after the dirty linen episode, she offered to leg-wrestle any onlooker or relative of same. She was aproached by a young man. They chalked up their monickers on a stone slab for a billboard: Malachi v. Esmeralda.'

'Esmeralda?'

'Her stage name.'

'Result?'

'Foregone conclusion. She won, of course.'

Snarling, Joey kicked at a stray cur snivelling at his feet for scraps and it scampered whining into a corner. 'Play to her ego,' he coached nasally. 'If she wants theatre, give it to her. Say the kid'll be bigger than that guy who came to town and juggled the sheep's eyes Saturday last at the inn. Look how she smacked her lips over him, how covetously her eyes sparkled at the idea of stardom. And, hey, say if she goes through with this, everyone in Galilee will hear about *her*, too.'

'I've said that.'

'And everyone in Palestine.'

'Do you think I'm stupid? It seems to have no effect.'

'Then try throughout the northern hemisphere.' Would that be enough for a wildcat? 'The whole world. For ever. Tell her that.' It was a crazy notion – for a wife (which is to say, a chattel) to go down in history for having a kid (which is to say, for doing her job) was, as they'd agreed, unlikely. But,

'If anyone's got the chutzpah to convince her, big G, it's you.'
J shrugged, and Gabriel, despite himself, blushed sheepishly.

The interesting thing that happened next is that an angel
appeared to Mary. He burst into her spartan room one
morning just prior to her work-out in a blaze of light
she wasn't used to seeing when Gabriel visited. The angel
wore raiment of a shimmering cloth that seemed to be made
entirely of nothing at all, or sky. He considered her calmly
and when he said, 'I descend to you from my dwelling place,
which is cloud nine, in the seventh heaven, bearing a gift
from the Holy Ghost which I am now about to deliver to
you in a way I think we're both going to enjoy', what Mary
liked most was the feeling of honesty about it, the complete
absence of the film or coating over the surface of everything
that lies give.

  The angel said that what was impressive about M (beside
her finely honed physique, which had, he admitted, drawn
many a gasp in the celestial land beyond the clouds) was her
energy, resourcefulness, goodness and stubborn, rebellious
originality. It was generally felt in heaven, he explained, that
Mary was the only person capable of dealing in a level-headed
and responsible way with a son who was a misfit by his own
choice, as headstrong and single-minded as herself. With that,
he conveyed to Mary the seed which would bud and sprout, in
due course, into a Messiah, and it wasn't like being prodded
by a cotton bud, it was like being licked all over by deliciously
cool tongues of flame. Mary was in rapture and, inside five
minutes, in the family way.

'She work out with those darn weights again this mornin'?'
  'Like no one you've ever seen. Gettin' livelier as the
years go by.'
  'Jesus is, what, ten now and Mary's –'
  'Mary's the captain of his rounders team.'
  'And you're stopping at the one, are you?' Gabriel stuffed
the corner of a leg of lamb into his cheek. He was really

getting to love that taste. Strange what you'll settle for. 'You're not going to nudge, nudge, wink, wink?'

'I beg your pardon?' Joseph glared hard at his companion. 'You know Mary doesn't, and never has, let me touch her.'

Gabriel smirked patronisingly. 'Well, it weren't me, boy. And if it wasn't you –'

'She says it was an angel. She says that's what this other angel Gabriel had kept telling her to expect for months.' The men eyed each other across the bench. 'One visit from the Holy Spirit, one child, the rest of her life lived in eternal blessing.'

'And virginity.'

'So she says. For now.'

Both men sighed. Having completed their repast, they rose and left the inn, outside which, inscribed in different coloured chalks on a granite slate, a message proclaimed: 'Here tonight! Esmeralda, the Bethlehem Basher, defends her unbroken record. Come and see the swiftest fists and trickiest kicks in town. Standing room tickets only left!'

At the end of the lane, Gabriel pounded his crook into the dust a couple of times and, shifting awkwardly, observed to his glum amigo, 'Well, at least we know the scheme wouldn't have worked. Like, who's heard of either of you, or the kid, now all the hoo-ha's died down? Who ever will? All you got left is the stuff those kings brought when the baby was born. And the only renown Mary has is as the Bethlehem Basher' – Joseph flinched – 'which won't run for long. She's getting older.'

Joseph gave him a half-arsed grin. 'Gotta go. Got to make an honest wage, since I couldn't pull off that dishonest one.' Slapping his friend on the back, he strode in the direction of his carpentry shop – outside which, amidst a gang of small lads playing rounders in the dirt, a woman with rolled-up sleeves watched his approach with indulgent, not unhappy eyes. Then she turned and swung a rough-hewn lump of mahogany, thwacking the ball and sending it soaring for miles, to a chorus of approving yelps from her son. As she did so, Joseph laughed.

'You're beautiful, for a strongwoman,' he called through the still, blue air. And when his wife smiled at him, her face seemed lit from inside with this weird kinda light.

The Gift

Zhana

Christmas Eve. Time to make merry. Time for eggnog and mince pies and all sorts of things that smelled sweet and tasted sweeter. But all Margaret could think about right now was finding her keys. Locking up safe and secure, herself and her new baby daughter, in the warmth of their new place.

The wind howled outside and her belly felt cold inside. The wind whistled and moaned around the corners of the building like a wolf freezing in the winter gale.

Nineteenth floor. Same as her age. Nineteenth year. She should have had so much to look forward to. But, looking down at the baby in her arms, she felt old. Old. Older than time.

Margaret wondered whether this child, this new life, had really come from her. Everyone said it had. Everyone said this was the being she had carried around inside her for nine months. Close to ten, really. The creature who had floated in a bubble inside her while its fingers spread and its toes grew and sprouted nails and it learned to flex its muscles. Slowly. Floating in the sea that was its universe. Her universe.

'Gloria', she had called the baby floating in that space below her breasts. Somehow, she had always known it would be a girl. 'Gloria', because her coming was a glory.

'We'll have babies. Plenty of them. Big, strong, healthy boys.' William had beamed after he slipped the ring on her finger. Boys. He had seemed so sure. It wasn't a real diamond. A zircon sat proudly on her finger, glittering in its gold housing.

'We can't afford a diamond yet. But I'ma do things right. I'ma buy you the biggest rock you ever saw. One day. We gon' live in a big ol' house with trees and grass and alla dat in the backyard. A place where the kids can play. And in the summertime, your mom can come and stay. And we can make barbecue.'

William talked on and on. He had it all planned. Margaret loved to hear him talk. Loved the fact that he knew exactly where he was going. And, of course, loved the fact that she featured in all his plans. 'Baby, we goin' straight to the top,' he always said. And she revelled in the golden beam of his attention.

When she got home that night, Margaret's mother and grandmother looked at each other and grunted.

'Mom, why you always gotta look like that?'

'And just where have you been?'

'With William.'

'With William.' Her mother's voice mocked her.

'Don't give the girl a hard time, Cheryl,' Grandma clucked.

'Mother, now you know that boy is no good.'

'Grandma likes William, don't you?' she said, grinning.

Grandma looked pained and sucked back into her mouth some of the words that were trying to spill out.

'I just think you can do better, honey. That's all.'

'But William loves me.'

A man loved her. Told her she was special. Sang her love songs from off the radio. Took her out dancing and bought her things. Noticed when she changed her hair.

All her life, this woman whom she had adored had told her to wash the dishes and hang out the clothes to dry and pick up her younger brother from school and give the baby a bath. All her life. All her life never had time for her. Never told her she was pretty. Never noticed her. Now, for the first time, her mother was giving her attention. Close attention.

'Are you pregnant?' Watching eyes bore into her.

'No, Mom.'

'You sure?'

'Mom, I told you. William's not like that. We gon' wait till we get married.'

'Honey,' Grandma interrupted.

'Why is it that you two are always so down on him. William loves me. Can't you see that?'

'Honey, just be careful. That's all I'm saying. Just because a man talks about marrying doesn't mean he intends to do any.'

'Look,' she said, stretching out her hand under their noses, her fingers spread wide, to display her new engagement ring.

'Is it hot?' her mother mumbled.

'Mother!' Margaret fought back the tears in her eyes and in her voice. 'Just because other men you have known may have been irresponsible, unreliable fools, does not mean William is like that.'

'Honey –' Again Grandma tried to interject, but her words were swept aside.

'Margaret, I just don't want to see you get hurt. Can't you understand, the boy is no good.'

Margaret felt a great crack begin to open inside of her, splitting her, rending her in two. Her surface erupted to expose her depths below, a deep cavern with torn, jagged cliffs on either side. Her left arm pressed against the ceiling while her right arm plunged into the floor. She would do anything, say anything, to stop this pain.

'You don't love me. You've never loved me.' All the pain spilled out of her mouth like lava boiling forth. 'Just because I have a man to love me now, you're jealous. You don't want anyone to love me. But you'll never find anyone to love you. No man would look at you.' Her words tumbled into the chasm that had opened up inside her. Desperately, she tried to fill the gorge with words. But they floated, tiny, into that great yawning gap and disappeared.

Cheryl, meanwhile, strode across the room and struck Margaret a ringing blow on the side of her head intended to knock her clear into next year, to wipe the floor and ceiling too with her carcass. But Margaret didn't feel it, so great was the pain inside her. The blow merely brought her back to the present, forced her to pull together the edges of the gap inside her so that it didn't show too much on the outside.

Cheryl's fist throbbing, she stared at her daughter, stared at the pain in her eyes, then leant forward slightly to place one arm around her shoulders.

'I love you, child. Don't you know that?'

But Margaret held her body stiff.

'I am not a child,' she stated flatly. 'And if you loved me, you would want me to be happy.' She turned and walked slowly, deliberately, from the room.

As usual, Cheryl didn't know what to do with, to or about her daughter. She only knew, at this moment, that she must not allow her feelings of rejection to show, must not show that she cared as her daughter moved away from her again.

So she called after her, shouted at her, screeched at her, 'Just don't come home pregnant.'

But she didn't get a reply.

'Jealous. Can you believe she called me jealous? Mothers aren't jealous of their children. What am I going to do with that girl?' As she ranted on and on, her mother said nothing.

It came as a surprise to no one but Margaret that she eventually found herself pregnant. And it came as a surprise to no one but Margaret that William disappeared, taking with him his dreams and his big talk and leaving behind only a gold ring with a zircon glittering in it.

When her mother threw her out, even Margaret wasn't surprised. She slept on a friend's floor, her bulk making that unbearable, while she drew her welfare cheques and waited to be allocated low-income housing. Meanwhile, the baby grew and grew inside her. She longed to have a place of her own, a nest to build, somewhere special. A place where she and her baby belonged.

The baby grew and grew, and so did Margaret. She had always been small, with short legs and fine bones, and now the doctor fretted about her gaining too much weight.

'You should only put on ten pounds,' he ordered, the mysteries of amniotic fluid and the growing placenta somehow escaping him. So Margaret went on a diet. As her baby hungrily devoured every scrap of food she swallowed, her own body cried out for nourishment. But Margaret was good. Followed doctor's orders. With a will of iron, she allowed herself only the intake permitted each day, her allotted 1,200 calories. Proud that she was doing her best for herself and her child. Looking forward to when, once the baby was born, the bulge would disappear and her body would shrink back to its previous slender shape.

Then, at last, the day came. Her waters broke and once again she felt as if she were being torn apart.

And then, this stranger, this glory. But it wasn't how she had expected it to be. This tiny new life with her perfect little fingers and toes, and her father's eyes. This miniature human totally dependent on her. Nobody had told her about constant crying when she couldn't work out what her baby wanted or needed, or when her baby was sleeping and the other babies' crying woke her up. Nobody explained to her why the bleeding got worse and worse, heavier and heavier. Until, walking around her new apartment, a new kind of pain struck her in the belly, bent her in half. Worse than the pain of childbirth because it brought with it no new life. Then the blood gushed out of her already weakened body and she and Gloria were back in the ambulance, sirens wailing, lights flashing. Like an action replay. Only this time there would be no new baby. Her daughter already lay next to her looking bewildered. This time there would be no more children. After the doctor took out her womb she felt that her womanhood was over, just when she'd been beginning to understand what being a woman meant.

She looked up to see her mother staring down at her, looking worried. Cheryl gently took her hand. 'I told you, a girl in your condition didn't have no business bein' on a diet.'

'Yes, Mom,' she said. But Mom hadn't told her. Margaret lay there, wondering who this stranger was who held her hand and looked at her with love in her eyes. And she wondered if she'd ever be able to look at her own daughter with anything other than fear, fear of doing something wrong, fear of damaging her, fear that some day the child would go off and leave her too.

And she wondered if her legs, which trembled and shuddered when she tried to stand, would ever be strong enough to hold her weight again. And she wondered if she were going to die.

But she didn't die. She recovered. Mother and baby were doing fine. And, since Mom insisted that they come 'home' for Christmas and was coming at four o'clock to drag them there forcibly if necessary, Margaret knew the only way she could make her escape would be to slip out at three o'clock, bundle up her baby in her arms, find a nurse to wheel her to the front door and somehow will her legs to carry her home.

No cabbie would take her to the South Bronx, even if she had had enough money in her purse for the cab fare. As she climbed out of the subway station to make her way to her new home, she remembered again, 'Yes, this is a bad neighbourhood. But it's all I can afford.'

The sight of bombed-out buildings, street after street of burnt shells of what had been homes and offices and shops, shocked her eyes yet again. She instinctively clutched the baby tighter. She knew it was a bad neighbourhood. But she had yet to learn that the fire engines screaming past, their sirens blaring, would wake her and her baby from their sleep, every single night. And she had yet to learn of the gangs of young men robbing and burning the neighbourhood and knifing and shooting other gangs of young men, every single night. And she had yet to learn of the horror of mothers tossing their babies from burning buildings, desperate, pleading, 'Please save my baby,' as landlords who could never make a buck from tenants who could not afford the rent set fire to buildings to collect the insurance money on them. Every single night.

She knew only that she wanted to get home. Back to her place. Their place. The only place just for them.

And now, at last, on the nineteenth floor, they were home. Away from nurses and labour pains, away from the smell of antiseptic, away from that certain smell of fear particular to new mothers.

It was Christmas Eve and they were home. Margaret stared at the newly painted walls. Home. To an empty place. There were no decorations. There was no food in the house. Maybe, while the baby slept, she could slip out and get a few things.

But where were her keys? In her confusion, she had put them down somewhere. Somewhere safe, no doubt. So safe she couldn't find them. Margaret became more and more frantic, worrying, flinging things about, hoping she wouldn't wake the baby with the noise she was making, hoping she could escape outside for a few minutes before those huge eyes began to open and that mouth began to bawl. Where had she put them? She searched and searched and searched again. Where were they?

Then a knock came at the door. Without regard to who might be lurking outside – an axe-wielding madman or some other denizen of the war zone that lay beyond – in her panic and frenzy, she flung wide the door.

There, planted in front of the doorway, stood a black woman of about the same age as Margaret's mother, with a very determined look on her face. Margaret felt a burning sting on her cheek as the woman's hand struck her hard across the face. Jarring her back to reality. Here she stood, in the doorway of her apartment, while her baby daughter slept. And there, gleaming in the woman's outstretched hand, were her keys. Her eyes began to water as she reached to grab the keys, almost taking off one of the woman's fingers as she snatched the keys from her.

'You left them in the door. *Never* do that again!' her new neighbour admonished her.

Dazed, and beginning to realise that the woman might well have saved her life, Margaret gulped, 'Thank you', and backed into her apartment.

'Merry Christmas.' The woman's voice floated down the corridor as Margaret shut the door and the baby began to cry.

Retablo

Eleanor Dare

She woke at 2.52 a.m. Sober as daylight. Alive as a newborn child. The green light of her digital clock glowed sharp and significant beside the bed. 2.52 a.m. It was numerologically portentous. Alex always kept a careful eye on these times; she was alert to the magic of bedside clocks. 2.52 a.m. She knew exactly what had to be done.

Out of the blue. Straight from the wind and piss blustering along the balconies. Don't look at me like that, Weary Face, you've got to believe this. It'll knock the stuffing out of you, out of everybody! *Retablo*. You know what that means? It's a Mexican thing – two-dimensional decorated panels all bubbling and alive. Figures dancing, devils riding bareback on devil horses, little red bastards hopping in flames. There'll be devils, go-go girls, shoplifting incidents, market traders, emergencies, dog's muck, an orgasm of human chaos, all the kids yelling, Christmas Eve desperation and vegetable barrels of exhilaration. I'll have a pint of London Pride, one Bells, no ice, and a bottle of ginger. Hello, Rita, how are you?

Calm down. These days all her friends were telling her to calm down. 'Speak slower, Alex,' they said – always Speak Slower, Calm Down. None of them understood how short life is, none of them understood what she was telling them about emergency, brevity, the *retablo*. About capturing everything in one epic image. How the rhythm of life was flowing through her veins. None of them could see that suddenly, this winter, Alex understood everything.

They sat in the pub together, crammed round a circular table inlaid with the signs of the zodiac. When Alex arrived she insisted that the friends reseat themselves so that everyone was placed beside their sign. They did it reluctantly, to please Alex, to protect themselves from the hours of playful pleading that would ensue if they didn't cooperate. They said of her, 'Alex is always happy', and asked enviously among themselves where she got her vigour from. None of them had known Alex Hill for more than two years, but all of them adored her. They were frequently irritated, though, by her boundless energy, especially when they were tired, and they were hurt by her frequent disappearances – outings they'd arrange which she didn't turn up for, and the ludicrous excuses she'd make next time they saw her.

Now it was Christmas and Alex was the only one among them who was enthusiastic about it. Over-excited about Christmas, not a woman of twenty-seven but more like a nine-year-old child.

'Look out of the windows,' she said, rushing up to them. 'You can see plastic cherubs above Marks and Spencer. Look at the Christmas lights, they are the most beautiful lights on Earth. I can't wait until Christmas. How many days did you say there are?'

'Nine,' they answered, gloomy and exhausted. 'Nine bloody days, that's all.'

'Nine!' said Alex. 'God, that's 216 hours. I wish it was Christmas today.'

The friends groaned, sipped from their beer glasses, discussed hot countries, overdrafts, ways of cheating the London Electricity Board, the things that depressed them about being straight, lesbian, celibate, until the conversation escalated into a symposium of despair – Murder Rape War. All set among the glimmer of pub tinsel, the clinking of beer glasses, Slade on the jukebox singing 'So Here It Is, Merry Christmas, Everybody's Having Fun'.

Finally they sat around the table in silence. A bunch of young men standing beside them looked down at the women with amusement. 'Miserable cunts,' they said, and turned their backs to gaze at the pub video.

The friends looked around for Alex, who had been playing on a computer game called Escape from Los Angeles. Now they missed her, they needed her impossible accelerated presence to buoy the evening up, to provide unwarranted cheerfulness in this grey season. One of them went into the ladies' toilet and called out for Alex, who often went in there for up to an hour to read the latest graffiti and add her own comments. But Alex had gone.

Out on the streets everything had turned a startling shade of viridian. Shards of green light danced in the bruised malachite of the early evening. Alex had trained herself to see only one colour at a time, to eliminate everything else, all other colours switched off. So now she was walking through a forest of green lights: fields in advertisements, jade lettering on carrier bags, emerald cars, pea-green shop hoardings, empty lager bottles placed at the side of buildings. She was hunting for colour.

She switched to purple, dazed by ianthine bulbs in the branches of London planes dotted along the high road. Mulberry and amethyst leapt from the shop windows. All was livid, violaceous.

The names of colours made her cry. She had never met anyone else so moved by them.

Everyone has to do a bit of stealing. Everything belongs to the inspired and dedicated thief, but, like the man says, who was it? I don't remember. Like he said, be careful to watch out for the quality of the merchandise. Certain things won't do. For example, there's no way I'm going to use those fluorescent lights in my *retablo*. Well, maybe the blue ones they have to kill the flies. Insectolocutor, that's what they're called, that's the tradename. It's like that book by Lorenzo Mattoti; did you read his book *Fires*? The one with the island and these leaf-creatures who capture all the sailors. How many days did you say there are until Christmas?

'Four. Will you come under the mistletoe with me?'

Alex thought lesbian nightclubs were a miracle. Alex thought the fact that there were other lesbians in the world was a miracle. Every time she passed another lesbian in the street, Alex gave herself a wish. It was like seeing a shooting star. A big section of her *retablo* was a nightclub scene with lesbian angels hovering above the dance floor. Some of the angels would actually be devils. Alex knew life was like that. She wanted to show everything, even the way this woman in the leather jacket was holding her, tenderly, her hands placed flat against the area where Alex's kidneys were. The way she stroked the inside of Alex's mouth with her tongue, tentatively, being so intimate and shy.

When they had finished kissing Alex asked the woman why the strobe lights cut up the motion of people dancing, why the red, yellow and blue bulbs moved in time to the music.

'How do they do it?' she asked. 'It's fantastic. Imagine if they linked up all the lights to our hearts, would you recognise your own bulb beating?'

The woman laughed uncertainly, decided Alex was on acid and disappeared into the crowd. Alex supposed the woman had only wanted to kiss. She carried on dancing for hours, especially mingling among the circles of women who wore bright-red Santa Claus hats. They were playful and tipsy. Alex thought, if people are prepared to make themselves look that stupid they cannot do much harm in the world. She would put the hats in her *retablo*.

East Lane in winter, two days before Christmas. The *retablo* was finished now, shimmering. Alex had sat in front of it for hours, basking in its magnificence. All life was there: popped Christmas bulbs, blackened chestnuts smouldering in street furnaces, fake snow sprayed into the corners of unwashed windows, cars stalling, couples arguing in department stores, lesbian angels, Santa Claus hats, pub games, pub fights, toilet graffiti, dog shit, Christmas puddings, violence, love-making, mayhem, market vegetables, Christmas trees and devils.

The *retablo* was finished and now it was beginning to frighten her. She had stared at it for so long that some of the figures actually began to move. Slightly at first, like the imperceptible shiftings of miracle statues, but then the dancing figures really did seem to dance, and the market stallholders seemed to weigh out the vegetables with the characteristic clunk of the weights on the scales and the women in the queues had pushed out their carrier bags to receive the vegetables. And, above all, the devils in the highest vaults of the sky seemed to be telling Alex that she was worthless and vile.

She ran out into the street. As soon as the frozen winter air slapped her about the face Alex remembered that the devil voices were in her own mind, as they had always been. She kept on running until she entered Walworth Road, slowed by its shabbiness, the sight of pit bull terriers shivering outside shops, weighed down by pounds of brass and leather. They all seemed to have one leg that shook pitifully. Above them the faces of a million last-minute shoppers all looked desperate – desperate for wrapping paper, for Sellotape, for bottles of whisky, turkeys, toasters, Brussels sprouts. She turned into the lane, wheezing for breath. Traders shouted out newer and lower prices, their voices impenetrable and befuddled so that they threw out words as if speaking in hieroglyphs, the language of Christmas – tangled and bloated with impossible expectations. At a lower level, the level of adult hips and knees, the faces of children looked out from winter hoods, ashen-skinned and urgent with needs among the toy stalls, the glare of sweets and stocking-sized objects. Alex looked out at the emptiness of the sorry park that spilt away from the lane, and thought only of her own emptiness, final and stone-heavy, of a vacant plot where all her hopefulness and energy had once been housed.

Wandering further down the lane Alex saw one of her

ex-girlfriends waiting beside the Sarsperella stall. She was terrified of being spotted because the woman would look deep into her eyes and see everything – her inside ugliness, the vacuum where other people had kindness and courage. Alex doubled back, crossed the empty park and walked down Walworth Road, until she stumbled into the first pub that presented itself.

It was like herpes. It was like a germ inside her that could never be shifted. She remembered vividly having thoughts of suicide at the age of eight. They came out of the blue. Carried on the wind, she supposed, just like her times of exaltation. Her sensational ideas.

Once when she went to the library, thinking there might be a book that could explain all this, the librarian, who knew her well, had laughed and said, 'Depression? You! That's a joke.' After that Alex decided it was best kept as a secret, because people would always laugh, they would never believe her. So she would always disappear, lock herself into the flat, sneak out to sign on. Hide if she saw friends, and receive no visitors until she felt well again.

Inside the flat it was hot, a constant piped temperature, but the doors ached with draughts from the wind outside, rattling and twitching in their frames. The whole estate groaned as the wind chucked debris along all the balconies, shook the flimsy trellising, scattered earth from Alex's windowboxes. She lay on the sitting-room floor, gazing up at the empty plains of the white ceiling.

When the wind died down she could hear the sound of a dog being tortured somewhere down by the garages. She was too fearful to go down there, to leave the flat. She was filled with contempt for her own cowardice and punched herself repeatedly across the stomach and breasts as the dog cried.

Later she could hear many footsteps along the concrete walkways, accompanied by giggling and singing, the rustling of small Christmas packages being carried between old neighbours. They seemed happy, but she could not believe they really were. It seemed like a fiction, like the three wise men and the star above Bethlehem. A myth like God himself.

When night fell Alex was terrified of being murdered. She lay in bed with a claw hammer held across her chest like a figure on a knight's tomb. Two weeks ago a woman had been murdered on the estate, her dismembered body found by a postman. Alex had seen the yellow police sign outside on the street and the striped ribbons twisted around the woman's flat like Christmas decorations. She had put the scene into her *retablo* and now she felt sick and scared just looking at it.

The devils in the *retablo* no longer talked to Alex – her own fears drowned out their whispered voices. Instead their hollowed-out eyes painted in yellow day-glo seemed to watch her, filled with hate, threatening and murderous. She rolled over in bed, turning her back on the *retablo*, still holding the hammer across herself, oblivious to the parties taking place all around the estate.

'I am a good person,' she whispered, not believing the words but using them as a spell to lull herself into sleep. After many hours of lying in darkness repeating the words, Alex hypnotised herself into insensibility – the deepest place she could run to: empty of dreams, inert and safe.

She woke suddenly at 3.56 a.m. Sober as daylight. 3.56 a.m. Christmas morning. Across the room the *retablo* faced her. The day-glo devil eyes flashed on in the dark.

'I am a good person,' Alex whispered, feeling for the hammer which had slipped down the side of the bed. The green numbers of the bedside clock glowed warm and significant as the time jumped from 3.56 to 3.57 a.m. Alex picked up the hammer and crossed the room. She knew exactly what had to be done.

I Wanna Hold Your Hand

Marijke Woolsey

Sue sat alone in one of the four booths that ran parallel to the bar. It was a Saturday night but too early for most of the revellers to be out, even this near to Christmas. Ron had bought the drinks over – dry white wine for her, whisky on the rocks for him – and then gone to the toilet. She'd never known a man pee as often as Ron. It was one of the things that annoyed her about him. She knew it was unfair and petty, and made a mental note not to comment on it.

She took a sip of her drink and surveyed the bar as nonchalantly as possible. A couple of middle-aged men in ill-fitting jeans and sports shirts propped up the mahogany bar at one end, their leather jackets swinging like hanged men from the backs of their stools. Three young men in sharp suits stood at the other end. The barman, like some Italian waiter in white shirt and black bow-tie, fiddled about with the ashtrays in the middle. Mainly she could see only the men's backs. When anyone glanced in her direction she studied the four ice-cubes that were melting in her wine. The last thing she needed right now was some plonker coming over to chat her up. Ron said she always was a flirt.

From speakers hidden somewhere above her head in the dark recesses of the low ceiling came music. The Beatles were singing 'I Wanna Hold Your Hand'. Sue sighed, relieved that they weren't playing an endless loop of Christmas favourites, and then she smiled. Years ago a boyfriend had bought her the single to make up after an argument. They were both teenagers and the relationship was a volatile one. She could still picture him – tall, slight build, dark-brown hair that was cut to stand up in two-inch spikes, like a Brylcreem-assisted hedgehog, big dark eyes with long black lashes. He always wore skin-tight, ripped jeans and T-shirts with offensive slogans like, 'Fuck off', or aggressive album covers from The Clash and The Sex Pistols. Giving her that record had been the most romantic gesture he'd ever made.

Ron sat down opposite her, putting his bulging Filofax at the wall end of the table. 'This place gets pretty loud later on but it's OK for now.'

Sue wished it was crowded and noisy.

Into the echoey hollowness of the bar came four young women, their bodies thinly sheathed in various Lycra creations. Sue watched Ron's face, the pale-green eyes scanning. 'Too young for you, honey.'

He smiled and his face lost its meanness with the laugh lines showing round his eyes. 'Thanks a bunch!'

'Any time,' she retorted, and waited for him to start talking business.

He sipped his whisky, surveyed the bar and said nothing. Sue noticed the taller of the two middle-aged men returning from the jukebox. It was one of the small, cigarette-machine-shaped ones on the wall with sections like Golden Oldies, Top Ten and Rock and Roll. She recognised the song from the intro as 'Yesterday' began to play.

As if this was his cue Ron began his prepared speech. 'We're both sensible adults. I see no reason for this to be nasty. I think it would be better to sort things out without going to court.'

'Cheaper, you mean,' Sue cut in.

He sighed and shook his head, as if he were explaining something to a stubborn child. She felt very watery, as if all the moisture in her body were rising up to her head, filling her eyes, nose and mouth.

The women at the bar turned in unison, laughing raucously. Clutching their drinks, they moved to one of the other booths under the admiring gaze of the young men.

Sue looked down at Ron's hands as they rested across the

table from her. He had square palms and short fingers with broad tips. He bit his nails – not down to the quick, but neatly clipped by sharp teeth. His fingers had travelled her body over the years, tracing her curves, into all her crevices, like a motorist with a well-worn A – Z. She remembered the way his hands looked after the birth of their first child. She had borne down, pushing through the circle of fire. She had squeezed his hands with a strength that made her tremble. When the baby, smeared with blood, had oozed out of her, Ron took his arms from around her. And as she sat down on the bedpan she saw his fingers, a purple-tinged white where she had cut off the circulation from the knuckles to the tips.

'When was it we stopped loving each other? Not after Ben was born, or we never would have had Josh, would we?'

'Sue. Please!' Ron rubbed the middle of his forehead, up and down with his fingertips. Then he took a large gulp of whisky that nearly emptied his glass.

'My round,' Sue said, and got up before he could object.

Standing at the bar, she studied her hands while the barman went off to fetch a new bottle of wine. Her nails were neatly filed, neither too long nor too short and painted a weak, pearly pink. Her skin was still soft, despite years of housework and never using rubber gloves. She wore only two rings. They sat together on the appropriate finger. The thin band of gold inlaid with three little diamonds and two tiny rubies, and above this the gold band with the star indent running round. She wondered at what point she should stop wearing these rings. What was the correct etiquette among divorced women?

The last bars of the song began to fade.

Sue looked across at Ron. He was older than her. He appeared more so tonight, slouched in the shadows. His hairline was beginning to recede, his waist to thicken. She guessed he was still attractive to other women. He flicked his wrist in a curt manner to check the time. She felt that familiar twinge of irritation, a split-second ache in her head. As she turned to cross the maroon sea between bar and booth, one of the young women glided in front of her. Sue watched as she sidled up to the jukebox and took up a pose in her psychedelic Lycra bodysuit, tiny stretched black skirt and carefully arranged limbs.

Sue put the drinks down, slid on to the velvet seat and said, 'It's simple. I get the kids and the house and you pay the maintenence. Let's say, £30 per week per child.'

'Be reasonable . . .'

'Reasonable!' she hissed between pale-pink lips. The silent wall of pain and disappointment sprang up between them. They retreated back to their dug-outs with their drinks.

A hard, throbbing dance record started to play and above the beat the lyrics chanted the merits of sex, lust and love. Sue smiled. The muscles of her small, round face relaxed.

'Very bloody appropriate!' Ron said, smiling back at her across the table and the crumbled wall.

'Do you remember that party in Stokey when we went upstairs and did it on that armchair on the landing?'

Ron laughed, a low, warm chuckle. 'How could I ever forget?'

Nine, maybe ten years ago, but Sue remembered the huge armchair. Its threadbare seat and the swirly celery-green material. The full skirt she wore with music notes and yellow roses on, spread out over Ron so no one could see that his flies were undone. They'd sat there laughing as she bounced gently up and down to the beat of the music coming up through the floorboards from the dancing room below.

They drank on in an embarrassed silence. In the corner of the bar stood a small Christmas tree. Sue guessed it was plastic, although it was a good imitation. It was lightly decorated with white and silver tinsel and balls. When the boys were little they'd decorated the tree at home as a family. For the last two years the boys had been more interested in playing with their computer and she did it alone.

'That's great, Mum.'

'Yeah, nice one, Mum.' The boys smiled at her over their shoulders.

'What do you think, Ron?'

'Lovely,' he said, never lifting his eyes from the pages of work that spewed from the briefcase on his lap.

Sue sighed. She ran her index finger round and round in the circle of wine that her glass had left on the polished wooden surface. She wondered if the hard young punk with the soft heart who'd given her The Beatles single had ever got married and had children. She hadn't thought she loved him then but he was her first proper boyfriend and he had always lingered at the back of her mind. A select, rose-tinted memory. Sue wondered if in years to come Ron might be stored in a similar section under the heading First Husband.

'I want to see the kids regularly.'

She brushed stray strands of fair hair from her face and fiddled with the pins that held the rest of it up on top of her head. She raised her eyebrows at him.

'I mean it. And I'd like us to be friends.' He glanced surreptitiously at his watch.

'Not keeping you, am I?'

Ron looked sheepish. 'It's business.'

'It would be.'

They sipped their drinks. The bar was filling up. Cigarette smoke hung like an evening mist in the still air. Bloody business, she thought. Half his mind always left at work. Christmas last year she'd hinted for weeks about the little gold earrings with the ruby and the diamond that would match her engagement ring. He'd bought her gold loops, very trendy. No doubt picked out by his fresh-from-college secretary.

Boxing Day she'd taken the boys to her mother's. Her sister had said, 'So, where's Ron?'

'Working,' Sue'd said, keeping her voice devoid of emotion. But she caught the raised-eyebrow expression that her sister threw to her mother.

'Get your feet off there!' she'd shouted at Ben, before fleeing through the french doors to the shaved lawn.

'Think about it, yeah? And give me a ring.' Concluding their meeting, Ron knocked back the end of his drink and picked up his Filofax. When he'd manoeuvred out of the booth he paused, waiting to see if she was going to leave as well.

'I'll stay a while. After all, the babysitter's booked till eleven.'

He nodded, then bent over and kissed her on the cheek. She felt a slight scrape from his stubble. It must be business or he would have shaved. She watched the back of his grey suit disappear through the gloom and bodies. It would be easier if he was a complete bastard all the time. If one of them had been unfaithful. If she hated him. Sue sniffed. Roxy Music began their cover version of 'Let's Stick Together'.

They had married in the spring. She wore a short ivory dress. Ron didn't stop grinning all through the ceremony. They couldn't look at the registrar because he had this lazy eye that kept slipping inwards and made them giggle. By the end of the day her cheeks ached from smiling. When they'd climbed into bed they lay very still together in the dusky orange-grey light that slid in around the edges of the curtains. They pressed their left hands palm to palm, ring to ring, before letting their fingers interlock and disappear under the duvet.

She chuckled, lifting her head back. One of the sharp-suited young men sauntering past on his way to the jukebox caught her eye and smiled back. He stopped in front of her. 'Is it a private joke or can anyone join in?'

Sue looked up at his smooth, oval face, his fair hair slicked back in a small ponytail. 'I was laughing at the song.' They were still smiling at each other. She could see his crooked teeth. She'd always had a thing about crooked teeth being sexy. It was something to do with a teenage crush on David Bowie.

'I'll put a record on for you if you promise to keep smiling.'

'"I Wanna Hold Your Hand". It's by The Beatles.'

He laughed. 'I know. I wasn't born yesterday.'

And they both laughed.

Chinese Baby

Carole Morin

A story in black and white.

He photographs Vivien's face, the handcuffs she gave him
for Christmas locked around a jar of Baroque cherries in the
background. As the camera stares, her kohled eyes watch a
spy thriller on television: a seductive Hollywood face in a tight
sweater, a movie of a book written by a man whose abandoned
wife has the same name as hers. He never divorced her. He
saved her from mortal sin. Vivien wishes she had a packet of
crisps. She wouldn't be able to eat them while the camera's
flash illuminates her spiritual vertigo.

They drove north to celebrate the end of the year.

Admiring their own purity, he stopped the car at a hot-
dog stand in Glencoe, listening for echoes of treachery above
the sound of *Lochinvar* on the radio and sizzling onions and
sausages.

Mustard and ketchup cure his hangover. He wishes his
camera wasn't in the boot.

Vivien lashes on lipstick, watching her mouth in a Chinese
hand-mirror, begging for a baby.

'A little one – for me to play with.'

They arrive in the village at midnight half-way through
Hitchcock.

The pub is deserted. A man steals Vivien's clothes as they
sit sipping rum and coke.

'Och, we should be drinking whisky,' Husband says,

relieved when they go back to the car that the thief has overlooked his camera.

'He must have been a transvestite,' Vivien says.

Joan Arch, kneeling on the floor of her rented room, semicircled by the tarot, manipulating the cards to win him back. His first photograph of Vivien is glued to her wall. She wills the destruction of her oblivious rival.

'Sexual jealousy,' she says aloud, 'is something I have never suffered from.'

She believes her voice when it's loud.

When she looks in the mirror, she imagines another's face, and whispers,

'I am beautiful without paint.'

She turns over the first card.

Poignards trois.

Three blades through the heart.

Joan Arch tells herself it's a good thing.

'Vivien Velvet has a face like a painted doll.'

Second card: *Le bateleur.*

'A symbol for him! He needs an excuse to see me.'

Joan Arch is tempted to call a female friend and discuss Vivien Velvet's obsessions: God, beauty, that Chinese baby.

But the third card, *Tempérance*, convinces her to go to bed.

Joan dreams that her cactus plant is sinking into marshmallow. There isn't a thing she can do about it.

Vivien and her husband, alone in their cabin in the mountains, swallowing oysters. Her thinking about that Chinese baby, wee Ming, a beauty gurgling under her dragon-decorated pagoda. Husband framing the baptism movie, wishing they had another crate of champagne.

'Do you think Joan Arch remembers us? We could ask her to be godmother.'

Husband laughs.

Vivien lies on the floor, rolling herself into a starched sheet.

Her husband kneels before her, searching for her hand in the folds of cotton.

She stays by the fire while Husband seeks photogenic deer. Avoiding realism, his camera attacks surreal clouds and invisible rain. He wants to make a movie starring Vivien's feet.

Her body is powdered, scented, waiting for clothes.

Her eyes are watching a serene face on the television that keeps changing.

Her ambition is a staircase.

Through the picture window, two wee things amble unseen along the mountain.

There are millions of mountains.

Vivien has eaten three tarts: lurid icing, fake cream. They make her husband sick. She used to eat them in the slums.

There was a baby in a big clean pram down the back.

Her brother's friend, Campbell, threw a brick on the off-white cover, soiling it.

Her brother sighed and threw a brick into the pram too.

Campbell lunged in a boulder.

Her brother had to find a massive slab.

The baby was smothered. Its mother took it to Australia: the cure in those days.

'I nearly fell out the window,' she told the local paper, who printed before and after pics of the baby's violated pram.

The baby's name?

Frère was seven; he didn't go to prison.

When he was fifteen he chased his best friend with her gun while Vivien was at school. Frère hated the best friend. His passivity drowned in cider, he had been unable to resist the air-pistol under his sister's bed.

After being shot in the bum, the friend barred himself in the fridge Vivien's mother had just bought. Mother had to find a man to demolish the door with an axe – the next-door neighbour of the dead baby.

Vivien's best friend had a round face. She dreamed last night that this ex-best friend had the fat suctioned out of her face, then held a cocktail party with tables and tables smothered with rich addictive hard chocolate-coloured slabs everyone was dying to eat.

Vivien's mum married a man. Frère ran away from home.
  Vivien said, 'Bandage up my feet, Mum.'
  'Why?'
  'I want them to be Chinese.'
  Joan Arch decides to dress up and walk to Scotland (she has no money). She sets off without make-up – to emphasise her beauty – and the photograph of Vivien Velvet in her pocket.
  'I'm Scottish too,' she says, waddling along the motorway, bare feet bleeding.
  'Vivien Velvet looks French.'

Dread is meaningless.
Tigers rip you apart.
It will be dark soon.

There is no cinema in the village. A fly goes to sleep in their cabin, then wakes up buzzing. Vivien imagines it's her baby crying. Husband has run out of film. He can't believe it – after what he packed! He is forced to drive into the city, along single-track road, he may not come back alive. He promises to bring her a virgin velvet dress.

Does she love me, he wonders, kissing her face goodbye. Is his rival the Chinese baby? She adores oriental philosophy, is addicted to leopard trim, loathes badly ironed labels. They prevent her from sleeping. Tossing and turning in the fevered bed, disturbing everyone. Black coffee is a drug. Detail is the key to her soul.

He is driving back up the mountain. His car is full of film. He loves his wife.
  He first saw her in a video. Her black and white face made

him want to leave the room – but he didn't; he sat there trembling (the way your foot does when you're talking to someone more intelligent).

What will happen if she doesn't have a Chinese baby? And it has to be a girl – a wee beauty, or it's no use it being a girl. She pretends to be capable of smothering an ugly child.

The road is blacker than usual as his white car climbs the mountain. Her favourite tape is in; he can't crash. More than anything he fears divorce. The city is only a hundred miles away. Catholics can't divorce. This Highland village is full of alcoholics who never walk on the mountain. Alcohol shrinks the brain. Mountains make you want to commit suicide. Water running under your house drives you mad! Never buy a house without dowsing.

Driving liberates the imagination.

Vivien Velvet is huddled in bed, listening to the blizzard, flicking through her scrapbook by candlelight. She's retired. The only camera that follows her now is his.

She expected the village to be more eccentric, more Gaelic, full of lascivious Bible-clutching puritans dressed in ankle-length coal-coloured robes. Coarse people have no souls. Catholics never divorce.

Suddenly a line of fire runs down her bed, turns the corner at the bottom, races along the foot. Vivien watches the flame until it turns another corner.

Snow covers her husband's windscreen. He is reluctant to destroy its pattern but is having difficulty seeing. Divorce is a mortal sin. She is small and beautiful; he needs to protect her.

Attracted rather than dazzled by his lights, the animal leaps in front of his car. Maimed, blocking the road: the enormous clothed rabbit forces him to get out of the car, drenched, swearing.

Close-up, the barefoot rabbit has the pouchy cheeks of a squirrel. It is Joan Arch, ex-girlfriend, martyr, feminist masochist.

'You still love me,' she says. 'You married her to escape my magnificent shadow. I can see it in your eyes.'

He drags her to the car. Her sanctimonious voice is drenched by the storm.

After saving herself from burning alive, Vivien has an impulse to vandalise something. Her tummy hurts. She wants a drink but her feet are bare. She is mourning the sapphire stud ring – lost, stolen, not with her now. She will never see it again for the rest of her life.

Vivien is naked when her husband carries dying Joan Arch into the living room.

'Exhibitionist!' Arch whimpers. 'All actresses are fakes.'

'Why are you dressed-up as a rabbit?' Vivien asks.

'I ran her over,' Vivien's husband says, handing his wife the white velvet dress. She pulls it over her head, grinning.

Arch crawls across the floor to where Vivien is lounging with a clear glass of iced water.

'You're laughing because you think you're prettier than me.'

Vivien had never thought out her philosophy, but ugly fools are no better or worse than sophisticated idiots.

'I am prettier than you,' she says.

'People who play games are . . . people who play games,' Joan Arch declares triumphantly.

A smile passes between Vivien and her husband.

'You don't love him!'

Vivien's husband tenses.

'You love yourself,' Joan Arch accuses her imaginary rival.

All this time Vivien has not thought about her Chinese baby, only her husband. He looks unhappy.

When they go to bed, Arch crawls into the corner of the room beside the burnished electric blanket.

Eventually they are unaware of her presence.

The holiday comes to an end. The Chinese baby will come with them next year. When they drive home, Joan Arch is in the boot of their car with a side of smoked salmon, what's left of those Baroque cherries, and the photogenic handcuffs.

A Trail of Rose Petals

Joan Anim Addo

Janie stared unseeing out of the window, her mouth set hard. Eyes, stony dark, caught the top of the overgrown rosebush and the shock of rioting colours thrown together. 'Hmmph,' she announced to the patchwork of crimson blooms bordered by vibrant pink, and then a harder 'hmmph' to the crumpled brown-paperbag faded deadheads.

'If is so allyuh want it . . . fine. I couldn't care less.'

Her dishevelled head, a mass of half-undone plaits, turned away as a sparrow alighting on a nearby shrub distracted her. The bird balanced delicately in the sun. Janie's right index finger beat a steady involuntary rhythm on the flaking windowsill. She returned a withering glance to two dying blooms side by side.

'Which of you is killing the other?' she wondered aloud.

'Is not so a woman must have to work hard, hard all she life. I stop.'

Her bare feet shuffled on the bathroom floor. It was gratifyingly cool.

'No more. I ent wasting my energies no more and dat is a promise. I free as the birds. Me life is me own. Let any adult in this house organise himself. Garden, you is my witness. He does sit right in that corner in the shade there with his newspapers then look around and sigh with satisfaction while I cooking. In the shade. Those days gone. End of an era. Is foolishness that make me don't think of meself before now . . . all this time! I start off thinking of he, then marriage, the children, now sense take over. Good.'

Somewhere a memory lurked that this was to be a pre-paratory day for something special, only more peaceful, with the children not there. But Alfred hadn't even noticed the children's absence.

'Good,' she shouted again. 'No more foolishness. Just watch me.'

Janie shivered. She was afraid. She did not know this newer self whose angry words uttered from her very own lips. A mild and only too compliant person she knew herself to be. But as she pondered, she tasted and recognised the fear she had always carried. She realised now that she had always been afraid. An image of herself as a child flashed before her, a small girl, sad searching eyes and so very alone. Janie sighed.

'Must it take a whole lifetime just to get to know myself?' she wondered aloud. She remembered then with dismay what day it was and a wave of exhaustion washed over her. She could hardly afford to indulge such foolish thoughts today of all days. New Year's Eve, some called it, but Janie, a creature of accommodation, who acquiesced to many customs, remained faithful to the significance of Old Year's Day, the day, and particularly the night, that saw the old year out. Tonight all who gathered at her house would share the special meal prepared by her to see the old year out and bring in the new. Janie would have to pull herself together. There was much to be done.

Alfred stirred in bed and rolled over to Janie's side. He tutted irritably. The sounds of his restless thrashings travelled so clearly, they could have been in the same room. Janie's face tightened. She worried whether she hated him and what was wrong with her to make her feel that way when so many had stressed her good fortune in having him. She had wanted to be looked after. She had wanted and given up on love, but above all she had never expected the volume of decision-making her life would involve. This morning, decisions, like the butterflies of her childhood, chased in and out of her head, settling at will while she watched, disarmed.

'Let the birds and the flowers and the beasts watch me.' Janie's voice rose determinedly up from the small window to the treetops.

'Yes, the beasts too. Even those stupid beasts that understand nothing.'

She turned in Alfred's direction and laughed to herself as she heard her mother's voice,

'If looks could kill,' echoed inside her head.

Thoughts of home lapped gently upon her consciousness. She set those thoughts aside, alarmed now about her state of mind. A woman's home was the one she made with her man and she had given up country, friends and a good many years for this. Janie struggled to attend to the day's business. She tugged at her dressing gown, intent upon starting the day's ritual ablution that would set her life again on its proper path.

Instead, her fists emphasised on the pulpit of the windowsill the futility of the existence of some dumb beasts she had encountered. It was warm work. Janie dredged the recesses of her mind. Somewhere there was a quotation from the Bible that she had learned as a child about such dumb animals.

It was while she searched that she was aware of a pounding on the bathroom door. She froze. Silence. Alfred's voice could be heard. Janie looked over her right shoulder at the door and sucked her teeth contemptuously. The glazing, patterned with so many startled eyes, distracted her. She addressed the garden again.

'Fifteen years I living in this family and I still can't go to the bathroom in peace. I haven't got young children any more and yet somebody's got to disturb me whenever I come in here. Is that a way that a person should have to live? All those supposedly clever men sit down in their suits making laws. Is there a law that says women, mothers, should not be disturbed in their bathroom? No. Too obvious, I suppose. It's only an abomination that's been going on since human life hit this planet. I know why they don't make those laws. Because those same grey-suited babies invade a mother's space same as any tiny babies.'

Janie walked with weary tread to the shower cubicle and deftly turned on the shower. As the full flow hit the tray, the hammering at the door intruded again.

She shouted, 'You can't come in. I am using the bathroom.'

She stepped into the path of the jets, still wearing her nightdress.

A female blackbird tightroped up tempo along the broken fence. Its long tail feathers beat time intermittently. Janie watched absorbed. She was aware that her hair was dripping. Absent-mindedly, she squeezed the water from her hair, making dribbles along the ledge.

'Where yuh mate?'

The blackbird twitched and hopped on to the flowerbed. It began a frantic calling dance in the wildest figure of eight. Janie watched, scanning for the bird's mate, as at a railway station watching out for fellow passengers. Suddenly her eyes caught her husband's down below.

'You finish in the bathroom?' He spoke through clenched teeth.

'You know what time it is? Twelve thirty. You sick or something? I'm coming up there.'

He struggled to control his voice in deference to the neighbours and his own needs for privacy.

Janie closed her eyes. She clasped her hands together, placing them as a pedestal for her chin. She gave way to violent shaking, echoed from her chattering teeth to the tips of her toes. Aware for the first time that her nightdress was soaked, she reached for a towel and wrapped it around herself. Her damp clothes troubled her. She had the uncomfortable feeling that here was something else she should be dealing with.

'Sick!' Janie battled with resignation. 'When you stay in bed till whatever hour is that sickness? Don't bother ask me any stupid question.'

The shivering resumed. Janie faced the self-contempt within even as her words flew at Alfred. She wanted to purge herself of this anger that had welled and welled and now threatened to drown her in unbidden images of timid childhood that reeked of fear. Her eyes narrowed in Alfred's direction. She read, in his face and posture, lack of understanding only. Disdain rippled in the high-pitched suck of her teeth. She looked away. He represented her failure. She focused on a more palatable subject. That lilac bush had been putting out leaves for a long time now and new shoots, but no flowers, she noticed. She wondered whether it would flower again, or if it had mysteriously given up its flowers.

'I'm coming up there,' Alfred declared again, through gritted teeth, his fury demanding a less public space than the garden.

Janie's eyes fixed upon that space where the topmost branch of their only tree met, in a mass, the pale sky, not now any shade of blue, more a shiny grey, for somewhere the sun still shone.

As the rattling of the doorknob and the banging permeated Janie's consciousness, she began her own slow dance around the room. She let the towel slide in an untidy heap to the floor and stood still, apart from eyes that darted to the door and restless fingers. Resolute now, Janie's fingers returned to the edge of the bath, where a clear plastic plant spray stood, its once-green lettering faded. She picked it up, still eyeing the door. Her fern, a solid reminder of home, nursed with determination, hung in green feathery stillness. She inched around the fern, spraying, spraying, restless hands stroking the damp fronds. Still the dance continued. She turned on the wash-basin taps and delicately cupped handfuls of water at the mirror, the pictures, the walls – a priestess offering incense. She began to shampoo her hair furiously, with an urgency greater than the renewed thudding at the door. Abruptly, she opened the door, a mass of dripping suds, the spray in her hands gripped like an offensive weapon.

'You can't wait to get in here, come.' A smile hovered about her lips. She glimpsed again this new person she was becoming.

Alfred glared. 'I am not in the mood for any of your infantile jokes.'

'Nor never has been.' Janie eyed him brightly. 'Go on, here's an invitation to some watery fun. Oh!' she mocked, covering her mouth. 'I said the wrong word. Fun to you is like the sign of the cross to the devil. It does make him feel very insecure.'

'Look, I work hard all week. I've told you before how demanding my work is. I don't want anything to worry my mind when I suppose to be resting. Besides, have you looked at yourself in the mirror?'

She ignored his question. 'Work?' she asked in turn. 'Work? You're the only person who knows what work is? Work is bringing up three children . . .'

'Not that again. Some women find child-rearing fulfilling.'

'Some women? Real women, yuh mean . . .'

'My mother had . . .' he interrupted.

'Not your mother again. I never met your mother but I'm certain I damn well know more about her than you could have begun to know. How can you know anything about having a child every year? How old was she when she died?'

'That is cheap.'

'As I was saying, work is bringing up three children and doing a paid full-time job and maintaining a small space that is still . . .'

'You're talking rubbish, and anyway you chose to work.'

'A familiar comment. Look at me and tell me what you see. Wife? Mother? Woman? You daren't answer. Who am I? Do you know? How many years have you known me? What differentiates me from any other woman you see out there, or indeed from the one inside your head? You can't tell me 'cause you don't know. I am not woman, that mythical being. I am Janie. Tell me about her. I have a real existence outside your head.'

'I don't have to listen to this rubbish. Besides, I intend to have some peace in my own house.'

'Peace? You've got more peace than you even know. I will tell you about the peace you have, because I can't expect you to have noticed. The children aren't here. They are on holiday. Hopefully they will meet some fun. F-U-N, which they have never encountered around you, you old goat.'

'You're being utterly ridiculous.'

'Tell me something I don't already know. Continuing to live with you for all those years, for the children, as you put it, is utterly ridiculous.'

'I suppose you think bringing children up on your own is easy. Hordes of women will tell you otherwise.'

'Don't you dare tell me about bringing up children, with or without a husband.'

'Don't I babysit for you? I probably do more . . .'

'Have you not understood at all that it is the quality of a relationship that may make a difference? Quality! It could make a difference for adults and, guess what, it can make a difference for children too.'

'I'm not standing here listening to your rantings all day. I'm the person who does the shopping, remember.'

'Yes, what is on the list only. Never anything else.'

The bathroom door slammed shut. So much more had been said than she had ever intended. Janie turned on the spray and took deliberate aim at the spot where Alfred's head would have been. She carefully doused his outline as she pondered the meaning of this new way of being.

'I made him disappear.' She swivelled her head at the mirror in apparent surprise. 'I melted him.' She laughed. 'I melted him.' The sobs shook her frame suddenly. 'I melted him,' she yelled, dissolving into tears over the basin, her head bowed as in prayer. She wept for the child in her who had always been fearful and for the woman who had carried that fear like a secret cancer.

When Alfred returned with the shopping, he rang hard at the doorbell as was his custom, having deposited the first bags at the door. With the second load of bags he rang again, with venom, and cursed at the absence of approaching footsteps. The bags piled up, nestling untidily against each other. Indoors, he shouted Janie's name repeatedly. The house echoed only stillness. The stomp of his angry tread, the slamming of cupboard doors, were to Janie as far away as the hum of distant traffic, and then further even than the droning of an aeroplane.

Janie listened instead to the twittering of birds in the bay tree nearby. She listened also to the rustling of leaves, the creaking of a swing in the garden beyond the new fencing, and intermittent children's voices. Her fingers slithered through the mound of velvet rose petals, in the plastic bowl on her lap, seeking the full roses left. She sat in her garden on the cool grassy step nearest the rose bushes. The dampness felt comfortable. She peeled her harvest of roses apart, liberating the petals, dropping the stems at her feet. She inhaled deeply into the bowl and closed her eyes, relaxing for a moment the better to comprehend it all. Confusion reigned within. She was in the garden. She was at home and yet not at home. She was herself and yet not herself; she was becoming some other and she was unprepared. It was not the right time.

She lowered her throbbing left temple into the bowl. Upright again, a small rainbow hovered inside her head. She wondered whether a dip on the other side would make two rainbows or one large one. The sunlight was a burnt caramel glow that she saw clearly through closed eyelids. Her right temple touched the cool mound of petals and she slowly raised her head.

'I don't believe this!' shouted Alfred from the doorway. 'Are you mad?'

Janie counted her beating pulse and breathed fear and panic

lest he had summed up only too accurately her present state – madness. Her eyes opened against her will. Alfred surveyed her, uncomprehending. Petals stuck to her hair and face. A washing-up bowl was in her lap.

'Are you mad?' he accused, in lowered tones, stepping forward.

Janie frowned. His habit of repeating himself infuriated her.

'I might be,' she said sharply. 'If so, what yuh gwine do about it? Take care of me?' There was silence. Alfred indicated the rose-petal-filled bowl.

'What the hell have you got there?' he demanded, his outrage overflowing.

Janie's eyes dropped. She gazed into the bowl. She shrugged her shoulders and yawned.

'Why are you sitting here on wet grass, barefooted in a nightdress at the end of the afternoon?' he hissed. 'We're having guests later on.'

'Guests?' Janie echoed. She could hardly have forgotten the ritual Old Year's gathering. In this place, home of sorts now, the New Year was invariably ushered in by a curious collection of exiles compromised by mortgages, expensive cars, a higher standard of living. She wanted no part of tonight's political discussions. She did not even want their compliments about her hospitality. She closed her eyes and considered how disappointing the reality of adult life was compared to the glimpses from childhood. Old Year's night had seemed like one long party. She knew now that it was effectively at least a day's worth of cooking and cleaning, mere chores after all, though once, a long time ago, the planning and cooking had brought excitement, like the wrapping of presents before receiving one's own. Janie breathed out long and hard.

'It is the year's end,' she thought, 'I am seeing it out in style.' Then she spoke in a calm voice which did not betray her bewilderment.

'When I pick up this needle and thread and this . . . case . . . it will look like sewing to you.'

'I don't understand why you should behave in this crazy way. If you want to do sewing, why can't you get dressed and do your sewing? It's quite simple. I presume you've got the meal sorted out.' Alfred muttered to himself as she walked away from him.

Food was of no concern today. It was the least of Janie's worries. More urgent, more terrifying, was what was happening to her. She was becoming another, just like that, in the miracle of an ordinary Old Year's day, and no one knew or cared except her. Alfred couldn't see and would simply not be able to cope if he could. The thought of him looking after her provoked an involuntary snort. It was her own decision to stop looking after him that had precipitated this crisis.

Janie eyed the returned blackbird in the distance, an idea taking root in her mind. Alfred was in her presence no more. She carefully set down the bowl.

'I am the storm,' she said, 'that passes in the night. I will go out with the old and the new will come in regardless. I choose the blooms that will tell of my passage. Snip, snip, snip.' She laughed bitterly. 'Some of this and some of that. Clip, clip.' She selected flowers from each section of the garden and laughed gently as she repeated, 'Some of this and some of that.' She tossed the cut blooms ceremonially on to the lawn, wondering whether every death was a new beginning, and for whom – the ones left behind or the one who goes?

When Janie stepped out of the front door in the early dusk, gathering already to cloak the Old Year's leaving, her eyes glinted steel. She shut the door quietly, with practised hands, and hesitated a moment. She considered in a flash the number of homes she had made in one lifetime, her children, her lack of friends that were just hers. She would have liked to take the car. She felt exposed, vulnerable. She held her breath. It would rain again tonight, she thought. It is humid. She scanned the street. It held an uneasy strangeness. Her uncertain steps descended the stairs. The paper carrier she clutched to her bosom spilled petals that trailed the length of her determined walk down the hill to mingle with the day's litter as the wind stirred. She stared ahead only, concentrating on the new start, the possibility of shaping new life, perhaps, out of what looked, for all the world, like certain emptiness. It grew darker. She never looked back and no voice asked, 'Janie, where are you going, leaving behind such a crimson trail?' And she expected none.

Wings

Julia Darling

First Mother trod on a nail and her foot went septic. Then she found a Bunsen burner alight in her bed, the mattress horribly smelly and melted. After that, it soon became apparent that Bliss was an arsonist and that everything would have to change.

It was a year of accidents. Glorious and sudden. She came to fear the smell of smoulder. There was too much suspense. By mid-year the whole house stank of sulphur. Casually ripped Swan Vesta boxes littered the hallways. The edges of the carpets were charred; armchairs scalded and frayed. The bedding had a smokey odour and the windows appeared sooty from within.

Mother wore a fire extinguisher clipped to her apron and converted the heating to electricity.

After the televised version of *Jane Eyre*, Bliss became extraordinary – fond of ceremony rather than mere flame. She began to dance around small pyres of twigs doused in paraffin, her flame-resistant nightie flapping in the sparks.

How she had learned these skills was a mystery. Mother believed in demons and alien infiltration. She was ashamed. She was afraid of Social Services and the women at the tennis club. She prayed to the stars instead. Babysitters were out of the question. Life was hot.

Bliss blossomed, lingering around the electric cooker with pockets full of crumbling firelighters while Mother eyed her with gloom.

Each day Mother and Bliss walked by the cool river. It was a slow walk, a walk that was intentionally dull, along a Tarmac path that opened into a wider dreary track; the river doomed, shrouded with exhausted trees, the ducks unintelligent. The path despaired eventually and became a car park. Here they turned and walked back through a nursery garden, pausing to watch rows of lettuces or broad beans in various stages of neat growth. Mother hoped to tame her child with these quiet forays into quotidian life.

But the year was not yet up. One afternoon, suddenly, a swan reared up from the river mud and charged at Bliss with watery venom. It wasn't as bad as it could have been. A mere peck on the arm and a white wing shutting out the sun. A few seconds. But Bliss turned quite white. White as a wing.

Mother was not good at sympathy. At home, the quietness hung like rivermist. Bliss thought only of the necks of swans and forgot fires. Mother sank into a smile and washed the windows.

On Christmas Day, Mother was nearly happy. A thin sheet of picturesque snow covered the hard earth. She had arrayed the house with daring paper decorations and even lit a candle in the front window, so passers-by could feel the warmth of Christmas time.

In the morning, Mother gave Bliss a doll with blue eyes that looked bleakly into the middle distance. Bliss gave her mother a picture in a plastic frame. She had drawn it herself. It was a grey picture of a river lined with poplar trees. Mother shed tears of gratitude.

Then, setting their presents aside, Mother suggested a walk before lunch, not noticing how Bliss's eyes also looked out into the middle distance. Bliss nodded. Secretly, Mother wanted to say a silent thank-you to the swans.

Once again treading the tedious river track, she pointed out how calm the swans looked, riding the dirty river upstream, but Bliss merely felt the inside of her pockets, and the red sulphur tips of loose matches. Mother said that swans belonged to the Queen, although no doubt they did much as they liked.

And Bliss watched the imperceptible falling of white snow,

and remembered the shock of the swan-bite – the sensation that had put out her fire, her passion. She raged against the boredom of her eleven years; the Formica of the kitchen, the pattern of the carpet in the living room, the neat dressing table in her bedroom. She felt sorry for the woman in the grey woollen coat who walked beside her. She was convinced that she wasn't her mother. A real mother would put her arms about her and love her. A real mother would never have called her Bliss. Something was terribly wrong.

It was uncharacteristic of Mother to lunge into the nursery garden and pick up a poinsettia. Bliss, left unguarded for a short wing of a second, flickered away, running to the shed that stood teetering on the edge of the river bank.

The swans gathered by the sluice, rummaging in the water with their necks curving dangerously, like snakes constrained in feathers. They looked up at Bliss with mean eyes.

Mother carried the poinsettia to the till and absently felt an empty breeze around her skirts. Then she smelt the old secure scent of paraffin and saw a twist of black smoke curling like a smile into the sky.

The shed burnt so quickly. Like a matchbox set alight, it tore into flame, falling down in sparkly gulps into the river, on to swans, on to beaks and white feathers. They flapped.

And Bliss roared with sad laughter at the swans' confusion. Matches in her hand. Hands in her pockets.

Mother just stood there, hands twisted around her red and green plant, sighing; as if a planetary omen had come true, as if all of Social Services and the people from the car park knew everything there was to know.

For a moment the warmth of the flames fanned her, and, as she dropped the poinsettia, she saw her past years like a great grey wave behind her, and knew that changes must be made in the wake of this and all other catastrophes.

Later when she told this story, many years later, she laughed and laughed until the tears ran down her cheeks.

And the only other thing to remark upon was the smell of Christmas dinner.

The Plot against Mary

Margaret Elphinstone

'I'm the Virgin Mary!'

Liz pushes her hair back wearily and lifts the lid of the spin-dryer. The kitchen subsides into throbbing quiet as the washing thumps gently to and fro among grey soap bubbles.

'I'm the Virgin Mary!' The high voice sounds shrill, still pitched to drown the noise of spinning clothes. Liz winces and summons up a thin smile as she turns to face her daughter.

'How nice,' she says, forcing enthusiasm into her voice. 'Would you like to hang some washing out?'

'I've only just got in.' Mary sounds aggrieved as she dumps her school bag and anorak on the doormat. She reaches across the washing machine for the bread bin. Liz stands aside to let her pass. 'Tell me about the Virgin Mary,' she says diplomatically.

'Well,' says Mary, restored to cheerfulness as she spreads margarine and peanut butter in thick layers. 'I have to wear my blue dressing gown and a white tea towel over my head, and a scarf rolled up to tie round it. Do we have a blue scarf?'

'No.' My daughter, my beautiful daughter, I'd clothe you in scarlet and other delights, and put ornaments of gold upon your apparel. Who would you be then? The whore of Babylon? I can't remember, though they taught all this to me. 'Did the Virgin Mary really wear her dressing gown?'

'Don't be silly, Mum.' Mary giggled. 'Though she ought to, oughtn't she? Like when we went to see Christine in hospital. When ladies have just had babies they always wear dressing gowns.'

'Women,' says Liz, exhausted.

'Women, then. And I have to come in with Peter Bradley – he's Joseph. He has to be because he's the only boy in the school as tall as me. And we knock at the inn door, and Joseph says is there any room, and the man says no, but he says you could take your wife to the stable if you like, and then we cross stage left and go down the steps.'

'And what do you say?'

'Nothing. I have to look exhausted and hold Joseph's arm. Peter doesn't like that. He thinks it's cissy.'

'And what do you think?'

'I don't know. Mum?'

'Yes?'

'If I was just going to have a baby, what would I be doing anyway? Would I be in labour?'

'Probably. Did you talk to Miss Gray about it?'

'Yeah. I said, couldn't I be groaning and clutching my stomach, wouldn't that make it a bit more realistic? Like this, you know.' Mary put down her bread and writhed in agony, rolling her eyes and moaning. The washing machine juddered to a halt.

'Mind out. I suppose the journey to Bethlehem stopped you practising your breathing exercises. What did Miss Gray say?'

'She said that was quite enough, and we wanted to approach this in a spirit of reverence.'

'Balls.'

'What, Mum?'

'Nothing.'

'You said "balls".'

'I didn't mean to. I just think a woman in childbirth deserves more reverence than a commercialised myth about a deoderised fertility god thrust into a misogynist mono-theocracy.'

'What you on about, Mum?'

'Nothing. I think you'll be a very good actor.'

'Actress.'

'Actor. Now, please hang this out, and we'll get the tea on before Gaia comes back from work.'

Three women at the table. The mother, the daughter and the mother's lover. Three persons in one council flat. The table is round, symbolising the infinite cycle of cooking, eating and washing up. The lamp above the table throws their faces into sharp relief.

'When I'm the Virgin Mary . . .'

'What's this?' says Gaia. 'What sort of ambition is that?'

'It's not,' protests Mary. 'It's our school play. I have to have a doll to hold, and we haven't got one.'

'Oh dear,' says Liz. 'Should we have?'

'I couldn't say I didn't. She just sort of assumed I would. Couldn't we borrow one?'

'Who from?'

'Couldn't you take Piglet?' suggests Gaia. 'If you wrapped him up well no one would notice he was a pig. His nose is the right colour.'

'If he was washed,' says Liz.

'I'm not sure Piglet wants to be the Baby Jesus,' says Mary slowly.

'How sensible of him. But mightn't he do the job anyway, to help you out?'

'No. People at school would laugh, and then his feelings would be hurt.'

'Yes, I can see that,' says Liz. 'Would any one of the other animals be prepared to do it?'

'Owl's beak would stick out, and Snake is the wrong shape.'

'Pity we haven't got a sacred cow,' says Gaia. 'Am I allowed to come to this play?'

'I don't know. It's supposed to be Mums and Dads.'

'I won't be hurt.'

'Well, I'd like you to, then you could look at me. You could pretend you were just my friend.'

'That won't be very difficult.'

Mary is always a long time in the bath, slow to start, slow to finish. Now the bathroom floor is a pool of water, the bathmat soaking, and a strange scent emanates into the hall. Mary follows it, exotic, draped in a scarlet towel, her fair hair dark with water and rubbed into a tangle. She stands in front of the fire, lets the towel slip and, naked, she dreamily brushes out her hair, watching herself in the mirror above the mantel-piece with absorbed appreciation. Liz watches too, covertly. This slow, dependent person who has insistently, persistently, modelled her mother's life into undreamed of directions, has been growing, has taken on a new private life and changed herself. Mary is tall and thin and slightly frail-looking, but her arms and legs are strong and golden-haired.

'We have a little sister, and she hath no breasts' – but she has, thinks Liz. She has breasts and she is nearly five feet tall, and still they expect her to sing 'Away in a Manger' with her blue dressing gown on back to front. Liz sighs, and goes to put the kettle on.

Gaia, sewing a scarlet suit for Piglet's Christmas present. Gaia, surrounded by patches and scraps of velvet, sequins and buttons, and swathes of wool of many colours. Gaia, choosing Piglet's buttons. Gaia, your love to me is wonderful, passing the love of – men. Gaia with straight dark hair gleaming in the lamplight, brown eyes frowning over her colours, mouth pursed in a soundless whistle. I know when she does that she's concentrating. Gaia, my love, if only there were no colder world out there.

'What's the matter?' asks Gaia, without looking up.

'How did you know?'

Gaia looks up and shakes her head. Of course she knows.

'I was thinking about Mary.'

'Yes?'

'And school. What they're telling her all the time, what they're teaching her. Taking away her power and her past. No more aware that she's a woman than they were with us. What can I say to her? How can I contradict it all the time? How can I make her understand without making her miserable?'

'You can't make her anything.'

'Yes, yes. But it makes me so angry. I can't do anything.'

'You do it all the time.'

'What?'

'You show her. Just go on being yourself. Go on being a woman like you are. Then you don't have to say a thing.' Gaia reaches out and delicately selects a strand of silk. 'Shall I put a woman's symbol on Piglet's pocket?'

'Yes. Why not?'

'Purple? Green? Blue?'

'Purple. The trouble is, when she's steeped in it all so young it'll just become part of her. And I don't know how to contradict it, because it's mine too. I've got "Away in a Manger" engraved on my deepest unconscious. I keep trying to learn women's songs by heart and a week later I've forgotten the words. How can I pass something on to her that I haven't got?'

'It's a brave thing to do, to reclaim a culture. Not easy. She's seeing you do it, and there's nothing better she can learn than that.'

'"Mary was that mother mild",' says Liz savagely. 'I don't want her to be anybody's mother mild.'

'Not even Piglet's?' enquires Gaia, as she stitches a purple circle.

Shopping in the Shambles, coloured lights and tinsel in ancient paved streets which have seen a thousand Christmasses. Small shops with Georgian windows full of arty trifles, design awards, pretty things, nothings. Liz buys two paper snakes on sticks for Mary and Gaia. She tests them in the shop and they coil and uncoil, dart at her face, alarmingly real. She stands between them, a woman remote and concentrated, a serpent in either hand. The shop is filled with coloured-paper lanterns, nothing substantial, no money's worth. Liz shudders, banishes daydreams, and pays for the snakes. The assistant wraps them in purple tissue paper and Liz steps out into the darkening street.

In the art shop she buys a paint box for Mary, twelve poster colours, and a sketch book. The day is greying, the narrow streets are lit by window light. The smell of real coffee permeates the alley. She passes the Oxfam shop again, and gaunt naked children gaze from the posters in solemn desperation above the painted eggcups. A hundred years ago they were real, pinched with cold and barefoot, sweeping crossings, begging in gutters, girls the age of Mary selling their bodies for bread. All cleared tidily away now to the further side of the world. Liz hesitates on the steps of the coffee shop, decides not to go in, and stands for a moment bewildered in the street, weighed down with parcels.

At the end of the alley the Minster towers black against the soft darkening sky. Slowly Liz wanders towards it, crosses the road, pushes open the small heavy door set into the great double doors.

The nave is roped off and she stands by the collection box, her knees against red rope, and gazes up to the painted windows opposite. There is a carol service, or is it evensong? She doesn't know, but the words are familiar.

> Unto us a boy is born,
> King of all creation . . .

The windows are beautiful, soaring upwards into the gloom. Early English. Phallic.

Round the corner faded banners of war hang, relics of righteous war against the infidels, the enemies of God. The crusaders came to this place to kneel in vigil and lay their weapons before the altar before setting out to liberate the Holy City. To sack Jerusalem, to lay waste cities more beautiful than anything yet made in Europe, to rape Arab women and to impale Arab children on the points of those Christ-blessed swords.

> In the name of the Father, the Son, and the Holy
> Ghost . . .

There is a noise of scraping chairs and feet, and the people start to sing 'Hark the Herald Angels Sing'. Liz shudders on her side of the rope. A righteous war. She imagines in the dim nave a gun-carriage, on it yet another phallic outline, a missile borne solemnly towards the altar. Uniformed men, some with dress swords some in long robes, process reverently beside it. 'We dedicate these our weapons to thy service, O Lord.' Made in your image, O male god of males.

> Born to raise the sons of earth,
> Born to give them second birth.

'Fuck,' whispers Liz savagely, and suddenly she turns on her heel and marches out, and the heavy door swings behind her.

The Virgin Mary is waiting in the wings.

The children are crushed close together. There is only a foot between the grey curtain which marks the edge of the little stage and the wall behind. They are hot, dressed in long, unaccustomed robes and clutching crooks and lanterns, cardboard gold, frankincense and myrrh. Their heads feel heavy with unaccustomed weight, cloths and prickly cardboard crowns. They breathe hot breath down each other's necks, and beneath their striped draperies their feet sweat in grey socks and school shoes. There is some shuffling and shushing, and the grey curtain sways.

Mary takes Joseph's arm and leans heavily. He grasps his staff and looks with sudden panic for Miss Gray in the wings opposite. She smiles nervously and beckons. Joseph and Mary step into bright electric light.

All Mary has to do is to follow him. He says his lines breathlessly and guides her to a school chair draped for some reason with a green striped towel. She sits, heaves a sigh of relief, free at last to look into the darkness.

Gaia and Liz sit about three rows back, not holding hands, thank goodness.

Becky is reading, 'And Mary brought forth her first-born son . . .'

Something prods Mary in the ribs, and she remembers, and takes the doll that a stray angel is thrusting at her. It is very hard and plastic and she glances unlovingly at it, while carefully cradling it in her arms the way Miss Gray showed her.

'. . . and laid him in a manger.'

She plonks it into the straw-lined orange box in front of her, as instructed. Its staring blue eyes shut with a faint click. She doesn't have to do anything for a while, as Gabriel is busy with the shepherds. Mary leans back and peers into the audience.

'For unto you is born this day in the City of David . . .'

Unto who? I thought it was supposed to be my baby. At that moment Mary catches Gaia's eye and Gaia winks.

The shepherds are standing solemnly before an angel in a white sheet and gold-sprayed halo. They glance round startled, their lines lost. The mother of God is unmistakably giggling. Five pairs of male eyes frown at her, and Miss Gray shushes impotently from the wings. Mary tries to swallow, and hiccups. She looks into the darkness and sees the serene reassuring smile of Gaia, then bends her head over her plastic baby, her bright face hidden. The shepherds ignore the incident and form a procession down stage right.

Liz stands on a chair in the doorway and sticks mistletoe to the lintel with Bluetak. Then she climbs down and surveys it, smiles, and moves the chair away.

When Gaia comes in she is waiting.

'Gaia, look up.'

Gaia looks up and laughs, and they move together under the mistletoe, and gradually their muffled laughter is lost in loving.

Last day of term. The classroom grows bare under their eyes as they take down the tinsel and paperchains, fold the crêpe paper, ease Sellotape from the windows, pile up the tissue paper stiff with glue. The collages are rolled into brittle cylinders, shedding coloured paper and glitter that crunches under their feet on the stained floorboards. Mary takes down her paper Christmas tree stuck with sweet papers in cut-out shapes, and collects her Father Christmas with cotton-wool beard and poster-painted red-lipped smile. She can hardly distinguish her own creation, her identikit Santa lined up with thirty-three others. She stuffs him in a Woolworths' carrier bag and rubs her eyes. The classroom is stuffy and noisy, the strip lights glaring. It smells of paper and paste and hot bodies. Her eyes get no rest from cardboard trees and synthetic snow, flat landscapes painted on dead walls, in metallic greens and hard bright blues. Mary looks outside into grey light, grey sky, lowering cloud. It must smell of rain out there. It'll be cold. She shivers.

Today they are allowed sweets and games. The dice rattle, fruit gums roll across the floor. One stops at her feet, livid green and sticky. Mary shuts her eyes.

'Would you like a bite of this?'

It's Peter – Joseph. Mary is startled. Boys don't talk to girls, don't offer their sweets. She is puzzled and wary, but she looks to see what he is offering, cupped in his two hands.

'What on earth's that?'

It is a fruit. Yellowish-brown outside, with a pointed end, but where he has slashed it open it is scarlet and juicy, plump and full of seeds. She reaches out with one finger to touch.

'It's a pomegranate.'

'Uh?'

'Pomegranate. It's my present. Want to try?'

It is ripe and solid, fresh and substantial in his hands.

'All right.' Her eyes open easily now, she is interested and curious. Peter flourishes his penknife, feeling suddenly powerful, and cuts off a piece.

The flesh is firm and juicy, but the seeds are bitter in her mouth. 'Sure you're meant to eat the pips?'

'Positive. There's too many not to anyway.'

A pomegranate. The best thing in this unreal day. I want to go home now. 'Thank you,' she says to Peter.

'All right. See you next term.'

On Christmas Eve, between midnight and one o'clock, animals can talk like people. Liz and Gaia have a cat, but she's asleep.

'Poor old thing. She can't be bothered.'

'She probably thinks there's no point trying to tell us.'

Liz sighs. 'I wish to God Mary would go to sleep. I'm dropping.'

'I'll do it for you if you like.'

'No, I'll wait. Then I'll have done it nine times. That makes a good number.'

'Tell me something important. That'll keep you awake.'

Liz chuckles, a little self-consciously.

'Yes, that one,' says Gaia. 'What are you thinking about?'

Liz laughs again. 'Okay, I'll tell you.'

'Good.'

'I'm thinking I'll change my name.'

'Good idea. I'd highly recommend it. What to?'

Liz frowns, stares at the fire, her face serious now, even formidable. Gaia waits intently, quick to sense her lover's change of mood.

The answer finally comes, spoken almost savagely. 'Lilith.'

'Lilith,' repeats Gaia quietly. 'Yes.'

Lilith stands up. She picks up a handful of gifts. 'I'll take these to her now. For the last time, I reckon.'

Mary wakes early, remembering through her sleep that today is all joy, all festival. She wriggles her toes and stretches, and sits up. Her stocking is waiting, full and bulging in the middle; she feels it pleasurably in the half-dark, then switches her light on.

This is a ceremony.

She arranges her animals, Piglet, Owl and Snake, and they watch from the pillow with unblinking eyes.

She sits cross-legged in the middle of the bed, the plump stocking laid across her knees.

She shuts her eyes and reaches in to take the first package.

Then she hesitates, opens her eyes and looks around the shadowy bedroom. Posters of horses, frozen in wild gallop, form a silent frieze around her walls. Mary looks at them, looks at the flyer for the Peace Group disco above her dressing table, at the photo of her grandmother on the mantelpiece. The morning is very dim and quiet. She whispers into the shadows, 'This is the last time.' She repeats it, her words slow and awed. No one has told her, but Mary has noticed that things change, and having changed a little, nothing is ever quite the same again.

She closes her eyes again and the ceremony continues.

Soon the gifts are placed in a circle round her, laid neatly bare. A tangerine, a penknife, a bag of mixed nuts, a snake on a stick, a pencil case, felt-tipped pens, a small carved box and a badge saying Girls are Powerful. Mary picks them up one by one, examines each deliberately, savours this moment which will not happen again. Then she gets up and drifts like a shadow across the hall to the toilet.

Lilith wakes as she has hundreds of times before, thinking she hears her child cry. She stirs, forces herself awake. But Mary is not crying, and now her shouts are exultant.

'Mum! Mum! I'm bleeding. Come here. I'm bleeding, I'm bleeding, I'm bleeding.'

The two women scramble out of bed, sleepy-eyed and clumsy. They run to Mary, standing there amazed, and hug her, laughing, there to reassure her and wish her joy.

Time on My Hands

Ann Chinn Maud

'Tuesday afternoon,' I read slowly, 'Beginning French, Ballet.' My audience sat quietly and comfortably in the warm Utah September sunlight considering these items, then severally shook their heads.

'No *Faatgwokwah*. Not English, not Chinese. No need other language!' Uncle said. Spanish, I noted, which he had claimed to speak fluently while married to his fourth wife, Carmen, had been demoted.

Moira O'Hallihan, pale, silent, as usual on the verge of tears, sat waiting — waiting for a class to be chosen for her, waiting for decisions to be made about her future life, waiting for her baby to be born.

Her elderly cousin Mrs Grey, twittering to no one in particular, pronounced, 'Ballet would be too strenuous for dear Moira in her condition.'

I continued, 'Cake Decoration, Latin American Ballroom dance . . .'

At this last item, Uncle Ralph made an unpleasant sound in his throat. I should have excised it from the list. It was at a ballroom dance class that Uncle Ralph had met Carmen, twenty years his junior, and married her. It was in another ballroom dance class that Carmen, now bored with her marriage, had met Wilmar and run off. I quickly went on. 'Car maintenance, Photography.'

Instead of commenting, Uncle held out his teacup expectantly. I stopped to serve refreshments. Uncle had cold tea from his Chinese pot on the mantel. Moira waited for the strong coffee forbidden by her obstetrician. Mrs Grey's choice was Ovaltine and I had a glass of V-8. I felt harried. My husband and I had bought a new "old house" when we had returned to Salt Lake City from studying on the G.I. Bill in Germany in 1958. With two children under five, the house to fix up, and my M.A. thesis to write, I had plenty on my hands without Uncle plummeting out of the sky like a burnt-out meteor, or, as Mama Georgia would have described him, a chicken coming home to roost.

Despite my retreat from things Chinese, my Heritage, perhaps in revenge for my desertion, would occasionally drop these remembrances in my path. One morning when I was scraping off wallpaper, I was interrupted by an insistent door bell and there before me, looking defeated, old, ill and laden with luggage, stood Ralph. He was a Wòhng, I was a Wòhng and the daughter of his oldest brother. So here he was.

'*Ngóh fàanléih ngūkkéi séi.*' (I come home to be cared for in my last hours, he extravagantly translated from the Cantonese later in the day.) The language didn't matter at the moment. I understood well enough from his appearance that his fifth marriage must have broken up and that he was here to stay for some time.

Colin, my English-born husband, more tolerant of the oddities of my relatives than I, positively savoured the stories which Uncle related his first evening there, particularly the one about the coffin.

'When I boy, older brothers buy two *gùnchòih* for Grandfather, *Yèhyé*, and Grandmother, *Máhmáh*, to be bury in when die. Get camphor wood all way from Szechuen. Expensive! *Máhmáh* say family cannot afford so much for *gùnchòih*, but really she pleased. She say to everybody all time, "See how our children care for us." But one day *Máhmáh* talk to old auntie. Man there painting two *gùnchòih* with special red varnish. Other times *Máhmáh* talk about that. This day when auntie say, "*Néih hóu hóu choi néihge jái gam yàuh sàm gam haau seuhn*" (You lucky have good-hearted sons show you respect), *Máhmáh* act funny. She start complain. "Oh, I tell them no make such big expense." Then, she say we not listen, not obey. Now she and *Yèhyé* have trouble to store *gùnchòih*, have expense every year to paint. I surprise. I say, "But *Máhmáh*, yesterday you say to Mr Lui, 'I have good sons. They take care of all death matters for us . . .'"

'Then *Máhmáh* shout at me. Say not interrupt when older people talk. Later *Máhmáh* explain. Auntie, widow. Only son die year before. Nobody left get *gùnchòih* for her. *Máhmáh* try make her think not important. But I stupid and old auntie, she go away crying.' Here he sighed lugubriously and shook his head. 'Before I no understand why auntie sad. Now I old man. Have no more wife. No children get coffin for me. I feel same.'

For some reason, although I sensed no hidden request in Uncle's story, I started to think about how to get him his *gùnchòih*. The difficulties burgeoned – the unavailability of camphor in Salt Lake City, how to locate a coffin-maker, where to store a coffin? We had only a small square of lawn and a patio behind the house. If we kept one there, what would the neighbours think? My imagination reeled with nonsensical elaborations on the theme, ignoring Uncle's voice rolling smoothly on to other tales, recounting other anecdotes. At that moment a *gùnchòih* of his own didn't seem to be weighing on his mind as much as mine.

Next morning, after the chaotic departure of Colin to the University and Sophie to nursery school, I sat down to write. I had forgotten about Uncle, so I was startled when around 11.30 I heard the characteristic slap-slap sound made by backless Chinese slippers coming down the stairs. There stood Uncle Ralph in the doorway of the study, stooped and unshaven in his pyjamas and bathrobe.

'*Ngóh lóuh lo! Móuhyuhng lo!*' (I am old! I am useless!) he declared, sighing heavily.

'Oh, Uncle Ralph,' I had never gotten over being awkward when speaking English to anyone Chinese. 'You're not old. You're only um-m-m fifty –' I paused and hoped my bid about his age had been low enough to be considered acceptable.

As it turned out, what I should have said was, '*Néih lóuh ah? Mhaih. Néih hóu hauhsàang.*' (Old, you? No! You're still a young man.) Later, Uncle had me practice this phrase over and over so I would be prepared if a similar diplomatic incident arose.

Still, I was shocked to see Uncle looking so droopy. He was rather vain and usually a very natty dresser. To show up dishevelled in his night-clothes clearly indicated a depressed state. I cast around in my mind for some way to cheer him up. Not necessary. Like most of my relatives, Fourth Uncle shared what I considered the gift of total *non sequitur*.

'Time eat breakfast now,' he suddenly stated. Being old and useless apparently did not dent the appetite. But before I could protest at the hour (it was almost lunchtime) or offer him corn flakes, he had vanished into the kitchen. A half-hour later, by which time Sophie had been delivered from nursery school, he had produced a delicious meal (his breakfast, our lunch): fried noodles covered with stir-fry vegetables with special Chinese mushrooms he had brought with him, and spinach and egg soup.

When I had finished washing the dishes after putting Sophie down for a nap, Uncle returned, dressed up as usual, and insisted on giving Alice her two o'clock bottle. Then he took both children out for a walk. By the time they came back for afternoon TV he had rendered Morris, my married name, into Cantonese (Mòuh) and taught Sophie to chant it with her given name (*Mòuh Ying Méi*). He paused to catechise me also, '*Gwai sing a?*', to make sure I could identify myself should emergency arise. He then handed me a bottle of fermented *dauh-fuh*, recalling to my memory my mother's stark translation from Cantonese of the name of this delicacy, 'preserved-stinking-bean-curd'. He recommended it as both delicious and healthy.

'Smell help make blood pure.'

After a week of this routine I sat down and took stock. I was ambivalent. Uncle was not really a burdensome addition to the household. Our new house was large, with four bedrooms – quite enough for all of us. Besides cooking, he positively enjoyed babysitting, which gave me more free hours than most young mothers have. He was companionable and told amusing stories. Colin liked him. I liked him. But he disturbed me too. Certainly, I could never meet his laborious instruction into Chinese ways or the Cantonese language without at least some faint resistance, and I found myself affecting to despise his opinions and values as a kind of self-protection. But from what? Perhaps the source of my irritation at Uncle's Chinese indoctrination was that it reminded me of my own incapacity. Besides, what need had I of stories of spirits called back into nearly moribund relatives or details of the grave-cleaning ritual of the Ching Ming ceremonies? These had nothing to do with my new way of life. Furthermore, I was irritated with myself for my own intolerance. I knew I was being both unfair and inconsiderate. Ralph was not taking his separation from his fifth wife, Bridgit, very well. Why should I begrudge him a little occupational therapy?

On the other hand, when he was not trying to resurrect my scanty Cantonese or get me to use Tiger Balm oil on Sophie's scraped knees, he spent the better part of the day following me around from room to room, complaining of his increasing infirmity and outlining his schedule of descending into the grave by inches, and this I found maddening.

'Mr Wòhng has so much time on his hands,' observed Mrs Grey timidly one day, the second week after Uncle Ralph's arrival. 'Do you suppose he might like to take one of those afternoon classes for adults?'

Mrs Grey, our neighbour from across the alley, had formed a secret plan. She herself had a young cousin living with her with whom she was trying to cope. She hoped that Ralph might be pursuaded to accompany Moira to a class, thus ensuring the girl a diversion once or twice a week. Moira O'Hallihan needed something to distract her. Scarcely twenty years old, she had arrived in Salt Lake City in early April 1960 from Belfast. She was a Catholic engaged to a Protestant and she and Patrick had decided to emigrate. Part of the reason was economic, but both they and their families were agreed that a 'mixed marriage' would be much easier to sustain in America. So Moira had come to stay with a distant cousin of both of them, a past model, the Roman Catholic Mrs Grey (*née* Colleen Kelly), now widow of an Oscar Grey, Orangeman. Patrick was to follow her in two months. Mrs Grey made plans for them to be married from her house. Then came the news that Patrick had been shot, followed by the discovery that Moira was three months pregnant. Moira had collapsed into a state of silent shock.

She roused herself enough now, when introduced, to say politely to Fourth Uncle, 'And would you be liking to go along to the classes, Mr Wòhng? Auntie is saying we should both be learning something new.'

He would. So there we sat this sunny afternoon in early September going over lists of offerings, comparing days and bus routes. After Volleyball and Chair-caning had been rejected, it was finally settled that on Monday and Thursday afternoons Uncle Ralph would squire Moira to Whittier School to a 'Sewing clothing for infants class', while he attended 'Woodworking workshop'. He would then escort her home. It was at this point that he added rather sententiously that having no descendants of his own to provide for him, he would use this opportunity to build his own coffin.

That evening at dinner when he described his plans to Colin, Colin lifted an eyebrow at me.

'Won't it be a bit of a shock when Ralph tells Mr Svenson he wants to make a coffin?' he said when Uncle had gone off to play mah-jong. 'Maybe you should go explain.'

'How do I explain something I don't understand in the first place?' I protested. 'When he gets there he might forget the whole thing and make a coffee table or bookcase like everyone else.'

Colin laughed softly. 'Or meet some people and find a new interest in life.'

'You don't think he'd want to . . . ?' I said as I prepared Alice's formula for the night. Providing a wedding for Uncle

Ralph would be even more daunting than getting him a coffin. 'His divorce from Bridgit isn't even final.'

'Just joking,' said Colin, and we tucked Alice in bed and sat at the piano practising anthems for the Christmas service. I forgot all about Uncle and his concerns for a while.

When classes began the only shock sustained was the price of wood for Uncle's coffin: $450 – walnut for the shell, cedar as a camphor-lining substitute. Mr Svenson, a stoic Swede, hadn't turned a hair at Uncle's purposed project. He had costed the materials and then instructed Uncle how to begin – learning to saw and prepare wood, to mitre and master the overlap, mortise and dove-tailed joints.

Uncle started by producing boards of eccentric sizes – 'shelving for house'. Our basement overflowed with shelves we weren't able to find places to hang. Then, after a while, this tapered off and with much grumbling about the difficulties of mitring, several failed attempts at picture frames, and a substantial contribution from his homework to our kindling box, he stopped bringing home wood or talking to us about what he was doing in class. Except that he continued to attend punctually, I might have thought he was losing interest.

He did seem to be pulling out of his depression. We had no Chinatown proper now that they had torn down Plum Alley, but plenty of gambling went on in private homes and in restaurants after closing hours, and wherever it was going on, Uncle Ralph was there. He had had a couple of offers of chef's jobs but had turned these down. His winnings seemed to keep him in funds. Woodworking class, mah-jong, babysitting and visiting Mrs Grey's kept him occupied. Whether the lightening of his mood came from spending more time in his gambling haunts or with our neighbours, I couldn't tell. Uncle Ralph had rapidly developed a very gallant style towards the two ladies across the alley. He honoured and respected Mrs Grey (Grey *taaitáai*), not only for her eighty years but more for her compassionate behaviour to her unfortunate relative. And as for Moira (Miss Mòh Wá), he felt very sorry for her indeed.

'She no more than child herself. How she look after baby? Who look after her?' he would mutter as he cooked extra portions of the choice foods for our dinner and trundled these across the yard.

'Grey, *taaitáai*, you eat this – make liver strong. Miss Mòh Wá, take more this dish. You eat for two, this serving for feed baby.'

He sometimes helped with their housework, since it was obvious that Mrs Grey was too frail to be adequately looking after herself, much less the very pregnant Moira. He was punctilious in seeing that Moira went to her sewing class. He reminded her to visit her obstetrician regularly and to go to services at St Mary's Church nearby. He decided she needed to make new acquaintances, so he got her to attend a Novena at the Cathedral of the Madeleine (Ralph claimed to know all about Catholicism because Carmen had been Catholic) and join some study classes given by one of the Jesuits there, a Father Michael Flaherty, and a professor from an eastern Catholic university, both of whom he seemed to know.

Halloween came. Colin carved pumpkins into grimacing jack o' lanterns and I made Sophie a witch's costume. With Alice as Wee Willie Winkie in her bunting, a night-cap and a cardboard clock hung around her neck, we went out with our candy bags and UNICEF boxes. At home there were pennies for the UNICEFers and apples to give away. Uncle fried doughnuts as an alternative and, leaving Colin on duty at our house, took a couple of dozen in one hand and three Kresses' plastic masks in the other and went off to Mrs Grey's. When the girls and I finally showed up there on our way home, Mrs Grey and Moira, masked as Snow White and Pocahontas respectively, and Uncle as Frankenstein greeted us and several other trick-or-treaters at the door. The kids eyed the three adults curiously. One forward boy of twelve pointed at Uncle's mask and piped up, 'Hey, mister, ain't you a little old for this?'

'Never too old,' Uncle replied promptly. 'In heart, I young man.'

'*Néih lóuh ah? Mhaih. Néih hóu hauhsàang,*' I responded instantly, parroting his earlier lesson in etiquette.

'You betcha, kid!' said uncle, his American slang startling all of us even further. But he plied everyone with dough-nuts and cider, and the kids left happy. Not me. Joking aside, I wondered. It was then that I realised how much time he was spending across the alley. I went home feeling distinctly uneasy.

It was Uncle, finally, and not us, alerted and promised though we were, who took Moira and Mrs Grey to Holy Cross Hospital when, just before Thanksgiving, the baby came early. We were at the Tabernacle at a Utah Symphony concert and arrived home to find a strange babysitter in the living room. Uncle Ralph had contacted her through the Yellow Pages, called a taxi and seen Moira and her aunt to the Delivery Room. He was waiting there now until there was some news, when he would call us. Late the following morning the call came.

'Baby Shòuh Bin, fine. Miss Mòh Wá, fine. Grey *taaitáai* happy.'

'Is it a boy or a girl?' I asked.

'I say name Shòuh Bin.'

Colin, linguistically intuitive, was on the extension and shouted down the stairs at me, 'I think he means Siobhan.'

Uncle heard through the telephone.

'That what I say. Little girl, Shòuh Bin.'

We rejoiced over Moira's baby with appropriate gluttony on Thanksgiving Day. Her delivery had been an easy one and after only a short convalescence Moira became more active than she had been before. When we visited her at Mrs Grey's after her return from the hospital she uttered a low rich laugh, the first of hers I had ever heard, when Ralph took Siobhan in his arms and tried to soothe her crying by rocking her back and forth, quite traditional except that he did it with the violence of a midway amusement ride.

As Moira became more outgoing Uncle's behaviour seemed subtly to change in reverse. He was preoccupied much of the time. He took to leaving the house early in the morning, reappearing only in late afternoon for babysitting. He began to receive official-sounding telephone calls, from Father Flaherty, from businesses, from (more outlandishly) the Parish Committee for the Propagation of the Faith. Whereas before he had relished these opportunities to converse lengthily on any topic at hand, he now gave terse and cryptic utterances and hung up as soon as he could. Even with the children he seemed abstracted. One morning when Sophie wanted to show him her success with the paper-folding he had been teaching her, he wasn't in any of the usual places. He was finally discovered sitting in the study, absorbed in calculations, with an L-square and compass tumbled on the desk in front of him. We located him through the clack of his abacus beads and the bilingual muttering of numbers. When I was clearing up the desk later, I found a book as well, *The Sacraments of the Church* by J. Flaherty, inscribed 'with gratitude to my friend Ralph Wong's interest in my life and work', and a model will among the papers. These could all have been interpreted as clues pointing towards a preoccupation with 'death matters'. But it didn't quite have that *feel*. Uncle seemed to be struggling with a different problem.

Of course, it was quite simple when I thought about it, really right up my sociological street. Uncle and I had the same problem. We were anomic. We had both lost our ties with our family. Not the small intimate family of the West – parents, siblings, a cousin or two – but the great network of kin stretching backward and forward in time, as well as laterally to those with the same surname, binding together all those of the same lineage. For a Chinese outside of this great affinal system there is no stability, no security and, in traditional communities, no possibility of physical survival. Of course, with the Chinese abroad much of this was modified, but it was still a very compelling force.

In falling through that net both Uncle and I had lost part of our identities. I, growing up in a predominantly American community, had come to an early realisation that my being 'Chinese' other than racially was a total impossibility. I gave up trying and had turned away from it. I had a new kinship now. My husband's world and our own family were enough for me.

But to Uncle, less Americanised and a generation older, such insularity must have made him feel inadequate, bereft. He might have been attempting corrective measures – to get back into the network or to found his own lineage, one which would attend to his 'death matters'. Perhaps that was why he kept on getting married. Of course, if he were to marry Moira he would already have a ready-made daughter. Had he thought of it like this too?

My preoccupation with the subject began infecting the holiday preparations. I thought about little else all the time Sophie and I were stringing popcorn and cranberry garlands to hang around the walls, and I mulled it over as I was making the caramel popcorn balls. Thanksgiving Friday I took Alice and Sophie to the Santa Parade. We watched in comfort from the front window of the China Tea Garden Restaurant on the second floor as the floats and bands and finally Santa in his sleigh passed down Main Street. Ray Hong, the owner, added to my discomfort by asking why Uncle hadn't been around to play mah-jong lately. After the parade we went to see Santa at Z C M I and, while we waited in line, I worried about what Uncle could be doing with his time. Colin was busy composing an organ voluntary for the Christmas service, so I generally tried not to distract him, but a week later I was so upset by an incident that I finally said something.

Wednesday had been designated for buying Christmas

trees. This year we would get a big one for us and a small one for Mrs Grey and Moira. Choosing was always a finicky business. Every tree on the lot had to be examined. Should we buy fir? (too droopy), juniper? (too bushy), Scotch pine? (branches too far apart) or get the same kind as last year, blue spruce (just right). I was unpacking the boxes of lights, tinsel and ornaments when I heard Uncle singing and, as I curiously approached the living room, some stomping sounds. The words were unfamiliar, but I recognised the song. Uncle was singing a Chinese version of 'Time on My Hands'.

Alarmed, I marched into the room. The dining table was littered with a sheet, a box of Kleenex, a wash-cloth and two baby blankets. A soiled diaper lay on the floor and in the middle of the room was Uncle Ralph, with a newly changed and gurgling Siobhan in his right arm. He was dancing with her to his own singing, '*Ngóh ji dím dáfaat / néih jōi ngóh dik . . .*' while administering her bottle to her with his left hand.

I must have looked very disapproving, but Uncle did not mistake the source of my displeasure, as an innocent might have done, for the mess around the table.

'Music for make baby sleep,' Uncle apologised instantly.

'That is *not* a lullaby,' I said accusingly.

Of course, he could just have been singing 'Rock-a-bye, Baby' in Cantonese to a popular tune, but I knew he knew the words of the song and understood me perfectly, because he answered defensively.

'Why not? Good music. Words right. I have plenty time. Baby in my arms. All hunkydory.'

As far as I was concerned, all was not hunkydory. Something was up with Uncle. Seeing him like that, almost as if the baby were a grown girl and they were dancing their wedding waltz, I was sure what he had in mind. No sooner did Colin get home than I tackled the matter with him.

'He wants to marry Moira. We've got to stop him,' I blurted out desperately.

Colin started by trying to calm me down. Then he considered my evidence carefully and logically. Next he pointed out practically that there would be unmistakable indications of a marriage afoot because they would have to go to California or Nevada to be married, the miscegenation laws being what they were. Then he said that there was nothing much we could do about it if they were determined, and finally drove me to exasperation with the cliché that it was really none of our business.

'Come on,' I argued vehemently. 'It's one thing for him to marry Carmen or Bridgit. They were nice, really, but we didn't know them before, so we could just be sorry that it didn't work out. We know Moira.'

'She's certainly had more than enough trouble already.' And from this economical judgement and his worried frown I knew that Colin felt exactly as I did. An unsuitable marriage followed by a divorce (if there could be a divorce since she was a devout Catholic) wouldn't be very good for Moira and it would probably kill Mrs Grey.

Christmas is a special time for me and I tried to make it so for my family. I had to get rid of my obsession about Uncle if the holiday was to go on at all. So despite increased calls from Fr Flaherty and more absences on Uncle's part and some new one's on Moira's, I firmly put my suspicions out of my mind. Colin and I were putting together a little grocery store for Sophie. He was making the counter and shelves out of apple boxes while I collected miniature products and bought a toy cash register and play money. I concentrated on that. I baked and stored up cakes and cookies, made fudge and assembled the makings of Christmas dinner. I made presents, bought presents, wrapped presents, delivered presents. Colin hung pine garland and Christmas lights on the front porch. We put up the tree with eight strings of lights, tinsel and ornaments. Sophie hung the ones down low on the tree. Alice and Siobhan, side by side in their carrycots, kicked their legs and cooed at the flashing colours. Finally, we put a white sheet around the bottom of the tree to cover the stand and piled the gifts on it. Whenever he wasn't recruited for putting something up, Colin practised carols on the piano in preparation for the midnight service at All Souls, so the house resounded with Christmas.

Just before Halloween Mrs Grey and Moira had taken to furious knitting. A layette, I guessed. But since the activity continued after Siobhan was born, I could foresee a certain number of bedsocks and scarves under the tree. Uncle went to and fro with large packages which were hidden I couldn't imagine where, since they were not in evidence in his room. He was being very mysterious, but I firmly put it down to Christmas and refused to speculate further. So the days passed by and the final gifts were put under the tree. We carried Sophie and Alice to All Souls Episcopal Church with us since Uncle Ralph was going to Midnight Mass with Mrs Grey and Moira and we came home past 1 a.m., heady with the service and music, and put the sleeping children upstairs before setting out the toy store under the tree.

We were a very large party for Christmas this year. Mrs Grey, Moira and Siobhan, of course, a student from England, a fellow cricketer of Colin's, and two Hong Kong students found somewhere playing mah-jong by Uncle. Sophie would have what Santa had left for her (plenty) first thing in the morning. The rest of us would wait until after dinner to exchange gifts.

What with jellied tomato soup, celery hearts, sweet pickles and olives, Waldorf salad, roast turkey, cranberry sauce, mushroom gravy, baked potatoes, corn, baked squash, sweet potatoes, Mrs Grey's and Moira's Irish Soda and Irish tea breads, Uncle's added delicacies of oyster dressing, stuffed-mushroom appetizers, and added to our pumpkin pie and plum pudding, a mandarin orange milk/almond junket dessert, not to mention providing Canadian Club for all the men to drink at dinner, after an hour and a half of solid eating we were all a little stunned.

We sat torpidly about while the children napped, watching TV or reading. I was shocked out of my stupor by answering the doorbell and finding a strange man standing there. Fr Michael Flaherty had come to join us in our after-dinner activities, an unannounced guest but obviously no surprise to Moira or Uncle Ralph. My dread returned. We were in for an announcement of some kind, it was clear. A conversion on Uncle Ralph's part prior to serious intent? Banns posted before going to California to be married? As always with Uncle Ralph, my imagination went reeling off unaccountably and I found myself remembering unlikely plots of romantic Fred Astaire movies: Uncle Ralph and Moira were secretly producing a musical; they would turn out to be brother and sister; she was a war orphan and he would adopt and educate her.

It fell to Colin to be sensible as usual and to nudge me into rushing around and finding a last minute gift for our unexpected guest. Fortunately, I had overstocked on ties and handkerchiefs.

Fortified by Charles Krug wine at dinner, eggnog afterwards and Christian Brothers brandy brought out for Father, we all grew very merry. First we sang Christmas music, 'Silent Night' and 'Jingle Bells', which everyone sang in their own language. Then came some English carols, Colin's and my favourites, and 'White Christmas'. Fr Flaherty, who turned out to be an 'Old China Hand' (he had escaped from the Communists by walking from Shanghai to Delhi) sang a carol in that dialect that none of the Cantonese speakers could understand, but everyone cheered anyway. I passed around chocolates the two Chinese students had brought as house gifts and likewise had showered on each of the ladies as gifts. Blind man's buff followed for Sophie, who enjoyed it because she thought the grown-ups looked so funny stumbling around. Everyone 'bought' groceries from her store and Sophie stood behind the counter with a butcher's apron on.

Uncle then presented identical huge lumpy presents to each child. Sophie laid waste to her wrappings immediately and we opened the others. He had given tricycles to all three girls no matter what their age. Sophie leapt on hers and pedalled off around the house. She ignored Uncle's more sober gift of fluffy dresses, this time chosen with the size of the recipient in mind.

The Hong Kong students had rallied in Chinese fashion and we were inundated with children's presents, rattles and pulley toys, a Mouse Trap game and stuffed animals. The more practical English Derek had brought Sophie a Paddington Bear book and the two babies English smocked tunics. Colin and I had exchanged our personal gifts in the morning and now received various books covering exotica from our own fields of research. The beauty and intricacy of the Aran-knit sweaters for Colin, myself and Uncle overwhelmed me. Mrs Grey and Moira had been knitting a lot longer than I had thought. We had ferreted out some Irish breakfast tea which was Mrs Grey's favourite and a warm bedjacket for Moira against the cold of midnight feedings.

The students and Father all received their ties and handkerchiefs with a show of surprise, with comments on the timeliness of the predictable bedsocks or mufflers (Mrs Grey and Moira), with thanks for the cartons of cigarettes (Uncle). Everyone had at least two stocking-stuffers and we all jabbered happily and admired each other's acquisitions. And it was at that moment of ease and contented relaxation that it happened.

Fr Flaherty stood up, gathering our attention together. 'I have a little secret to be telling you, which is why I've come along tonight. Happy I am to be sharing it with so many friends.' He beamed and drew from his despatch case a bottle of Jamieson. 'It calls for a toast.'

Full of foreboding, I got tumblers. Father made a great display of passing around the whiskey, then moved over and stood next to Moira. He smiled down at her and she blushed suddenly as he said rather surprisingly, 'I'm sure you all know my brother James.'

Most of us having never laid eyes on Fr Flaherty before this evening, I thought this was rather a presumption.

'He good teacher! Nice man!' recommended Uncle. 'Play good mah-jong,' he added, giving me a clue to the origin of the acquaintance – undoubtedly another 'Old China Hand'.

''Twas he that was visiting me on his sabbatical from Notre Dame this fall,' continued Father. 'And would be here now but for the sad business at his University. Especially at this time.'

Why in time for Ralph's engagement, I wondered.

Father nodded to Uncle Ralph, who dashed out and returned dragging an extremely large and heavy Christmas parcel.

'Now, Miss O'Hallihan wants Siobhan baptised as soon as may be, so we'll not be waiting for James to come back,' Father continued.

I looked at Colin and Colin looked back at me. I was more confused than ever.

'We'll not be waiting for the engagement to be announced before the baby is christened,' Moira spoke up suddenly, as if trying to make things clearer.

So it was an engagement. I had been right.

She blushed again and went on. 'Auntie will be one godmother, I'll be the other and Mr Wòhng has agreed to be godfather, and when I asked Fr Flaherty he said he thinks that is only right. After all Mr Wòhng has done for us, James agrees. James is most grateful.'

My head was beginning to ache.

'Excuse me,' I interrupted firmly. 'Just what does James Flaherty have to do with all this?'

Fr Flaherty, perhaps a little miffed at being preempted by a mere girl, took the announcements back under his control.

'Why, he and Miss O'Hallihan are engaged.' He seemed shocked at my incomprehension. 'A toast. To the happy couple, the baby and the godfather.'

Uncle Ralph pushed his parcel in front of Moira.

'For baby Shòuh Bin from Godfather,' he said importantly.

Mrs Grey helped Moira open the gift. She was beaming and obviously in on everybody's secrets.

Slowly the large object was divested of its layers of wrappings and a fragrance filled the room. From the bottom appeared the sight of a curved piece of wood and then a straight backboard which seemed to be attached. What was appearing was walnut and cedar wood and beautifully finished. I couldn't identify it. Surely not Ralph's coffin. But no, it was the wrong shape and size for that.

Then Colin said, 'Ralph! It's a cradle.'

'You betcha! This number-one American cradle,' he proclaimed proudly. 'Teacher show picture, say Shake people make like this.'

The student guests, who had been consigned to a purely background role during the various revelations, now crowded forward to praise and admire. Mrs Grey filled the cradle with pillows, sheets and a coverlet which she had hand-sewn and knitted.

I was curious enough to ask very directly, 'What happened to the coffin?'

'No can make so many joints. I decide more important baby have bed – change coffin to cradle. Take lots time, hard-work, but it one swell job, no, yes?'

'One swell job!' Colin and I agreed absolutely.

Ralph went off to the study, the designated nursery for the evening, to get Siobhan. The happy godfather-elect carried the baby into the living room. He smiled broadly at us all from between Moira and Mrs Grey as he leaned over and laid the baby in the cradle. Then, straightening up, he said to all of us, his voice full of satisfaction and accomplishment, 'Now I have godchild, I no worry no more. When she grow up, she get me *gùnchòih.*'

The Cooking of Heart's Content

Mary Ciechanowska

I was on my way out to some brisk Saturday shopping at the after-Christmas sales when the phone rang; I almost didn't go back. A good thing I did, though. It was my nice cousin Caroline and I could hear the panic, even on a crackly line. 'Their cooker's *powered by electricity*!' she was screaming. 'I've not used one of those since Mother's. Tell me all about it, Jane. It's really old, like yours. They've taken Jim's Mum round the corner to look at a sheltered flatlet so we've got about twenty minutes. Come *on* Jane, *give*! I need it *all*, the whole picture. My entire reputation in this neck of Putney is hanging on it.'

I told her all I knew, being especially careful, of course, to remind her about the anticipation thing, the need to adjust the heat, up or down, a little in advance of requirements. I have always been a cheerfully electric cook myself but Caroline is one of those for whom gas is the one true way. She talks about the alternative in the language of the divorce courts (and she should know), calling it insensitive and unresponsive and tending to brutality.

Caroline is a dedicated cook and an even better friend. She sees the two pursuits – of flavours and relationships – as closely intertwined. Cupboard love's an accolade, in her book. So when, the day before this phone call from a strange kitchen, she had met her middle-distance acquaintance Fiona in the high street and heard about the less than festive Yuletide that Fiona and Jim had just had – how Fiona had spent the run-up to the season at Jim's hospital bedside watching him recover from a heart attack, and then Christmas itself, and after, in a very hard bed of her own, having injured her back the day after Jim's homecoming, rushing downstairs when the doorbell rang to stop him getting there first and, for all she knew, stuck right back into some kind of coronary-inducing work problem with his unfeeling partner, Harold, out there on the driveway and (Fiona felt) the cause of the heart attack in the first place – she (Caroline, my cousin) had offered to pop round one night and cook them a nice dinner. Not a Christmas one exactly, she couldn't face another of those just yet – the one that had just been and gone had embroiled her, for the sake of their adolescent children, who had passionately pleaded for parental symmetry on Christmas Day at least, in fourteen hours of enforced *bonhomie* with their father, otherwise (and rightly) forbidden the family home. But Christmassy enough, the thought would be there, a few festive backward glances; she'd a box of crackers left she could take round and some draggled paper hats and a Chichester Cathedral cassette.

Fiona had smiled politely, said, 'Oh, how lovely, Carrie. I'll talk to Jim about it', and hobbled on her way (her back had got to her walking), and Caroline had dived into Cato's after cat litter, thinking it would probably never come to anything really, and then not thinking about it any more at all.

Fiona had phoned that night. 'Jim thinks it's a lovely idea! And his mother's coming to stay tomorrow and she's looking forward to it too. Do you think we could make it tomorrow? You buy all the stuff for it, and then I'll pay, of course? I insist, as it's to be eaten at my house. You as sort of providing-angel guest.'

The prospect of Jim's mother worried Caroline, fleetingly. She doesn't like to cook for people she doesn't know; it is almost a sort of contradiction in terms, she feels. She had met this woman only once, and only for a moment, while carol-singing for charity the year before. The old lady had been a pointed, papery face just above Jim's shoulder, in the shadows of his hallway, while Carrie and her fellow carollers had stood on the bottom doorstep, quaking their way through 'Silent Night'. It's not good, I know from my own experience, singing something simpering in the full glare of a hall light while a group of other adults have to stand there too – except its their hall and *they're* smugly inside it, so near and yet so far away. It would be so much easier after a couple of drinks, but then you might get your sibilants sloshed up and shame the charity of your choice. So you go for it, take your money and run, and all that Caroline knew about Mrs Baileybridge was that she was old, and papery, and pointed, and kept fairly late hours.

And also, from Fiona, that the old lady too had a heart. It was a condition that ran in Jim's family. Two hearts and a mending back, thought Caroline. Not a robust situation. After Fiona's call she phoned me for a chat about it, decided on the British Heart Foundation cookery book, and went to bed early.

As it turned out, that first sighting of Fiona's cooker was the last bad moment. The call to me, and a few judicious notes on what I'd said, jotted down in the spare pages of the new Sainsbury's diary, cleared all panic away and Caroline set to work with her usual aplomb. She was whistling, she says, by the time her three hosts got back. In the fullness of time she produced an asparagus and potato bisque whose ferny subtleties would have been a fair way to heaven even by the standards of real angels, though she says it herself. Jim said its smell was so good no taste in the world could possibly live up to it. And then, after his first spoonful, simply looked at Caroline for a long moment and said, 'I was wrong.' Fiona kept repeating, 'Delicious. Simply . . . delicious', in that dreamy, almost drugged way of the truly moved. The unelderly speed at which old Mrs Baileybridge saw off her bowlful was, Caroline felt, praise enough.

Next came the grilled butterflied leg of lamb with lemon and garlic, with crunchy green beans laced with that lovely East European crumb sauce (not quite British Heart Foundation, but Caroline's son's Polish-born supply teacher's and very low in cholesterol) and sautéed mushrooms and rounded little new potatoes. Jim and Fiona sniffed the air in joy when it was brought on and during the first few forkfuls a transported silence reigned.

Then, gradually, a lot of lively talk broke out about textures and nuances and good old-fashioned tastes and the best bits of people's lives that the food was putting people in mind of. As there always is whenever Caroline cooks; she always says that really good table talk should do that – start with what's on the plates and lead off everywhere. Fiona was rolling her eyes with the joy of eating such wonderful food, in her own home, that she hadn't had to cook herself (even if she could have), Jim was going at his plate with a pink-cheeked gusto he hadn't felt for food since before his attack, and old Mrs Baileybridge seemed to be having the time of her life. Caroline, sitting beside her, noticed that her pink tissue crown was trembling slightly, like a happy little leaf, with the excitement: such lovely things to eat, after all, and so much company, and a glass of wine – the doctor said it was all right, in her case, taken carefully, she said, though Fiona kept looking doubtful and saying, 'Are you sure, Mother?' Jim drank almost nothing.

Finally, they reached the pudding, a light yet full-flavoured low-calorie strawberry mousse made with flown-in fruit from Harrods that, Caroline knew, would taste all the better for being their first and last for months. She began to feel that it was safe to let creative tension drain away and, having flourished this final concoction on to the cloth, settled back into her chair with all the sensual pleasure of the suddenly relaxed, saying, 'And this, like everything else you've had tonight, friends, is no threat to anyone. Everything has been out of my good old heart-fancier's food book. Every last crumb.'

At which precise moment Mrs Baileybridge keeled over to just enough of an angle for a few grey fronds of front hair to tremble gently above Caroline's pudding. No one really noticed much, at first, because, as I said, it was a very subtle sort of almost-normal position she'd keeled to, not an outright horizontal, and she had dozed off for a moment or two a couple of times earlier in the evening, and then come to with an endearing little jerk to tiptoe back into the conversation. So at first only Caroline was worried, by the hair, in her low-calorie mousse, trembling, and the talking went on.

Then Caroline stopped in mid-sentence, and they all stared at the old lady's hands. They had started to move, like mice, in little hesitant runs, first back along the table-cloth, then up their owner's chest to her face, where they crept about the mouth, making worried, fingertip excursions, as if to make sure that the mouth was all still there. The last time Caroline had seen that had been at the sudden passing of her banished husband's father. She didn't mention that now, of course, but she did suggest a doctor, in that always very useful, tight sort of tone that hints at secret technical know-how and gets itself obeyed (I used it myself, when the cat caught fire at my mother's). Fiona limped off to the phone.

Meanwhile, Mrs Baileybridge came round, opened her eyes for a moment, said, 'Au revoir, but not goodbye, Jack', and then, '*Hasta luego*', and then closed them again, this time laying her head fully in the mousse. It looked bad; Jack, Jim muttered, was his dead father. (Later, he explained that his parents' happiest times had been on package holidays, and that this had lent a touristic turn to the language of most of their everyday exchanges.) Caroline noticed that the hair had given up its trembling, and that seemed to be the clincher.

It all speeded up after that. The physiotherapist from across the road came round with a flushed new husband and a dressing gown with a hole across the back, revealing 'Squeeze Me Till Morning' in purple glitter-print, which wasn't very funny but made Caroline suddenly long to roar and roar with laughter; shock, she afterwards decided. The ambulance men arrived and, later, a doctor, and all that was needful was done, and soon Mrs Baileybridge's body was on its way to the morgue, or wherever, while her presence, in the room, seemed realer than before, and very peaceful, residing chiefly in a half-drunk glass of wine and a still grey hair in a pudding plate.

Caroline felt bad about it all for some weeks, until Fiona rang up and said she wasn't to. It could hardly have been the food, could it, and anyway, it had been the loveliest way to go, the best sort of Christmas present you could get, really, at that age; they should all be so lucky, when their time came. Hadn't Caroline noticed how Christmassy the room had seemed to become, after the ambulance had left? Full of gratitude, somehow, as if someone, somewhere, were saying a really heartfelt, 'Thank you, it was just what I wanted.' Honestly! Hadn't she noticed?

Come to think of it, Caroline told me later, she had.

Brightly Shone the Moon That Night

Fiona Cooper

The wind woke her at six, hustling the leaves on the trees, still green in November. It gusted into every overhang of concrete, whistled down the brick funnels on the tall building where she lived. It was a busy, no nonsense and let's be having you noise. Out of her window she watched the wind whisking fallen leaves along the gutter into pavement-high stacks of yellow and brown.

The letterbox clashed and no letters came. All that hit the floor was a glossy leaflet inviting her to discover the magic of Christmas at the local hypermarket. A plastic Santa was sledging across the snow-white surface of a cake. Two candles burned. A glass of untasted wine stood at the side of the cake, a round red something at its base. What was it? A baby Edam? A pantomime bomb? She started to feel uneasy.

She could save up to eight pounds – *yes! EIGHT pounds in this Yuletide Bonanza*. On the next page, another plastic Santa stood holding a walnut. He was on the edge of a table, covered with *festive fayre*: plates of beef and suntanned turkey, roast something scaled like an armadillo and studded with cloves; bowls of nuts, fruit and cream. Paper streamers like coiled fuses were scattered between the plates and wine bottles. Three dull-red baby Edam bombs sat among the gleaming cutlery.

She could garnish a turkey with chestnut stuffing balls, bacon rolls and pork cocktail sausages. *A tender turkey is traditionally the main attraction of a Christmas dinner*. Perhaps she'd find a flashing neon sign to stick in the parson's nose.

Big Turk and the Cranberry Kids. The Gobbler That Ate Paris. A Sizzler for All the Family.

And why not, jabbered the leaflet, over a half-dozen slices of cheese, why not seize the chance to educate her jaded palate from the dazzling display of continental wizardry to the rear of the store?

A tureen of Technicolor sprouts looked at her smugly. Carrots curled into roses and golden hedgehog potatoes sneered: *Make this the year you take on the challenge of making vegetables more interesting.*

Oh, yeah?

Well, why stop at a syrup glaze?

Perhaps she'd slide a copy of *Oliver Twist* into the bread bin and have a chinwag about good old Charles with her toast. The *Encyclopaedia Britannica* could be rehoused in the vegetable rack. Awesome aubergines! Did y'hear what that broccoli said about the theory of relativity? The potatoes could cast an eye over Jean-Paul Sartre and reshape their destiny: no more chips in her house, *non, non,* my dear, *pommes frites.* Should she play them music? Tchaikovsky for the onions and perhaps Stravinsky for a truly surprising vegetable stew. If she left a dictionary in the cupboard, by heaven, she'd get a good game of Scrabble out of a can of alphabet soup.

Dates should be stuffed.

She squared her jaw and nodded. The next time barmy Billy at The Queen's Arms asked her if she was keeping company, she'd tell him to stuff it. With the finest marzipan. They used to call it marchpane. Bread like what you only eat in March to keep the Lenten hunger pangs at bay.

Page three's Santa had one of the sinister red bombs over his shoulder. It was smooth and round but he carried it like a sack. Wassail, wassail, come buy our ale. Save your pennies and don't forget the Rennie's. Beer and whisky make your old uncle frisky. Dry Martini, put on your bikini. A schooner of sherry will help you feel merry.

The last page was a dragon's hoard of chocolate and toffees

and gateaux. Santa lugged a foil-wrapped truffle as big as himself. The baby Edam bombs were replaced by chocolate beans with ice-skates and cheeky little smiles. *Just for a treat, why not try something sweet?*

Suddenly she was ravenous, and she knew for sure that the cupboard held only labour-intensive proper food. She wanted a snack and no washing-up.

It was a strange day outside. The wind was moving everything along like a nervous policeman. A drunk and disorderly can clattered on a grating. Torn Sunday colour supplements made eyes at her from the railings. Someone had left a leather jacket on a fence and it was eleven in the morning. Why on earth had no one taken it? She wondered whose it was and what had happened to them. She feared something awful, for it hung like a rag and people walked past it without looking twice.

In the high street a golf umbrella flapped on the pavement, blown inside out, one spoke standing up like a mast. People walked round it, a pram wheel caught it and dragged it a little way. The cars were slow with the cones curving out from the pavement. A cardboard box banged her knees as she blew across the road to where an old lady was hopping on the spot and poking at a plastic bag on her foot. The wind had turned it into an octopus and the old lady muttered, 'Oh dear, oh Lord, oh good heavens, what a nuisance.'

It was one of those days where she stood staring at corridors of soup cans, dithering between chicken korma and coconut or sweetcorn and satay. If you bought six cans, you got one free, but she'd only wanted tomato anyway and that wasn't a part of the offer.

Then, in the queue, she was in front of Min and Joe. Min was blind and rode in a wheelchair, her head lolling to one side. Joe worshipped her and piled bunches of flowers on her lap. He bought her doughnuts and cans of Carslberg Special, and they picnicked on the pavement and he sang to her. He sang 'If You Were the Only Girl in the World' and he sang 'Help Me Make It Through the

Night'. Min ate her doughnuts and beat time with her can and laughed at him.

'I love her,' he told passers-by. 'She won't marry me, but I'll never stop asking. I worship her and she won't make an honest man of me. She's my girl.'

Min had a wire basket on her knees. They were buying Eccles cakes and treacle tart and currant buns and iced tarts with bright-red cherries on top. Joe had a bottle of Thunderbird too and had already opened it.

'You are my sunshine,' he sang and up-ended the bottle. Min bit into a macaroon.

She liked Min and Joe and so she walked past the news-agents smiling, without noticing until she was almost at the next newsagents, which ran out of her newspaper by ten in the morning. Only today they still had a copy. The woman was at the other end of the counter, weighing bull's-eyes, and called at her just to leave the money. The sun rolled a watery silver eye behind the clouds.

In the street she caught the smell of tar. It drew her to a big yellow truck, where a dark scarf of smoke tugged across the pavement. A flame roared under a black bucket, clean blue like a blowtorch clinging to one side. Around and above the treacly bubbling, the wind shredded the flame orange and mauve and tossed the tatters like an angry juggler. Sparks flew and vanished. Five workmen stood near the heat, bare chests sweating, shoulders goose-pimpled. She could suddenly see years back, when her dad took her to smell the tar-bucket. She had a bad cold and he'd dressed her in layers of clothes so her coat buttons bulged and her boots were tight and hot.

'Smell that and tremble, pet,' he said, holding her hand. 'Clears your lungs out.'

'Be my *love*!' bellowed Joe, behind her, steering Min round a dustbin. He parked her outside the betting shop and lit her a cigarette before he went inside. Min's head was almost level with her shoulders and she smoked with a long black cigarette-holder. Her hat was a stained velvet Rembrandt, fruit lurching over one ear, and her dark glasses made her a parody of Bette Davis's cameo wicked eccentrics. She sat crumbling pastry in her pink gloves and the wind blew ash and tiny sparks from her cigarette.

Four doorways down two little girls were hollering, 'Penny for the guy'. They gawped at Min and asked each other what on earth it was. The taller one shrugged and started to push their guy away. Who's going to give money for a stuffed anorak and football tied to a pushchair when there's Min, life-size, with cherries on her hat, puffing clouds of fag smoke in a real wheelchair?

Joe came running through the plastic curtains waving a slip of paper and a handful of notes.

'Minnie Mouse! Ten to one!' he shouted, and waltzed his darling Min and her chair so fast that they crashed against a bollard.

'Wheeeeeeeee!' yelled Joe, jumping on to the back of the chair, and he and Min whizzed down the street, bumping on the uneven paving slabs.

'Pair of daft kids!' said the old lady who'd freed her foot of its plastic octopus by now.

'That's Min and Joe,' said her friend. 'It's lovely, the way he takes care of her. They'll be drunk as lords by teatime the day.'

When she got back to the flats, the leather jacket had gone. Someone set off a rocket over the green, and red and blue sparks hung for a moment against the thunderclouds then vanished into thin air.

Later that week, three children knocked at her door.

'Silent night, holy night,' they sang and one of them collapsed giggling.

'All is calm, all is bright,' chanted the other two, hitting their friend.

'Round yon virgin mother and child, holy infant so tender and mild, sleep in heavenly peace, slee-eep in heavenly peace,' they finished with a high-speed wail.

She gave them a pound. It was, after all, the season of goodwill or something very close.

A Lost Present

Joanna Rosenthall

They had still been in the car when they met Mr Hyman. He was a short, rotund figure in a black suit, shiny and worn at the cuffs. He wore a yamulka. She felt a rush of warmth towards him because he was looking after Mike. He ran over to the car and waved his arms impatiently until Sydney rolled down the window. He was so small he had to bend only a little to stick his head through.

'You aren't the people to see Mike Freize, are you?' They both nodded, anxiously. 'Well you're far too early. He won't be here until 11.15. He's still at the other hospital.'

'That's okay, we'll wait. It's only half an hour; we wanted to be here early.' He had sounded rude, brusque, but she tried to ignore the tone he had used, intent on reassuring the man. He seemed to need it.

'And did you know that we have to have time after you've been, so you'll have to be quick? He's not the only one you know.' Sydney started to wind up the window, to shoo away the little man.

'We'll be back in half an hour . . .' The car's engine drowned Sydney's words as they swung round and crawled down the hospital lane, coming to a virtual standstill for each speed bump on the way. They had half an hour to kill.

The short windswept walk chilled her. She was clutching Mike's present in her hand. She had considered leaving it in the car but it was too precious. Wrapped in fuchsia-pink tissue paper, it had a huge white shiny bow. Their daughter had also insisted on little silver stars all over the front. It looked ridiculous and bright. She was ashamed to be carrying such a cheerful-looking object. What would Sydney think? She turned to look, but he was walking doggedly ahead. He didn't seem to have noticed.

Each time her eyes strayed from her feet she regretted they'd come. The small green common, surrounded by windows winking with fairy lights, smiling Santas and stick-on snow. They should have stayed at the hospital and sat in the car.

Mike hated Christmas. Over the ten years they had been together he had tolerated it, but this year had been different. Turning forty had changed him. He had protested, 'I'm not going through that charade again. First of all I'm Jewish, I've got no genuine feeling for it. Secondly, Jesus probably was a good guy but Christmas has nothing to do with it, and all this stuff they push at you, all the hype and the consumption, it stinks, I can't do it. I'm changing this year. I don't want a tree, they're tacky, and I'm not getting any presents.'

She had resented being lumped together with all that. 'Of course it stinks. But there's more to it than that. I love giving presents and I've got all my memories from being a kid. You're Jewish, but I'm not. The fairy lights and Father Christmas coming down the chimney, you can't rob the kids of that. It was magic for me. Why can't it be for them too? What's wrong with it? We can do it our own way. It doesn't have to be all bad.'

She had bought him a small present. It was a book of poems by someone they both admired. A beautiful poet who was a magnificent mixture, full of feeling, yet sparing nothing of the world's cruelty and pain. It was a present that she hoped would help him understand what *she* meant by Christmas.

They had rowed. It was running round her head, filling it. It was only a few days ago, or was it weeks? What day was it? She must ask Sydney. What day was it? The colour drained from her face. She felt heavy or was it light? Why had he been so angry? Why had she? Was there more to it? Why did he have an accident now? Was it the car? Had he had a drink? No. They had said he definitely had not been drinking and there was no other car involved. She had an uneasy sense – it was too hazy to question but powerfully there – that somehow she was responsible for this. She hadn't managed to keep him here.

She suddenly felt very strange, as if her whole self had tucked itself away inside her head. She couldn't speak, her feet felt awkward, large and unsure of any direction. There was nothing inside telling them what to do.

She brushed Sydney's arm. She couldn't manage anything else. He looked sideways and took her arm. 'Back to the car,' he said rather aimlessly, although realising that was what she needed. He repeated it several times whilst she walked alongside, like a child who had been told exactly what to do.

She sat in the passenger seat, the present balanced on her lap, half hidden under her coat. Sydney held the steering wheel. It was cold. Time was very slow. The silence became tingling at first, then unbearable. She turned her head slowly and looked at him. She had never seen him slumped like that, his head at a funny angle, leaving an ugly old man's ledge at the back of his neck. It was horrible. Being Mike's dad he had become a kind of a parent to her too. He was a quiet man, his eyes telling you he understood more than he ever put into words. But now he couldn't meet her face; he was completely still, inside himself, unreachable. Only his hands were there, gripping the steering wheel, holding on very tight.

Not speaking, the half-hour passed slowly. Eventually he started up the engine. They returned to the hospital, the nurses' home on the right, more fairy lights, even glimpses of a Christmas tree within, no people. No people on Christmas Day; they were all doing something else. She remembered Mr Hyman's harsh-sounding voice from yesterday. 'Christmas Day? Of course it doesn't matter, it's a different religion.' She had felt punctured and vacant. There was nothing to say. The canteen on the left, continuing on until the road seemed to stop, instead turning sharp right, down the back of the boilerhouse and so narrow that it could hold only one car. She felt panic rising within. Could there really be a Jewish place where Mike would belong in amongst so much Christmas? So much tinsel and fairy lights? It helped her understand a bit more about what he had been saying. How Christmas wiped him out. He was different. He had wanted to be himself.

When you couldn't go any further the mortuary was directly ahead, an L–shaped building. The long part for Gentiles, and the short, squat bit nearest to the road was for Jews. Why did it remind her of concentration camps? It was a small unadorned brick building. Over the door there was a Hebrew inscription which she didn't understand. She wished she could ask Sydney what it meant, it might comfort her, but the silence had become hard and unbreakable.

They sat in the car until Mr Hyman drove up slowly in a large car, a shooting brake.

'Don't look,' Sydney whispered, his eyes darting anxiously towards the mirror. He had parked facing away from the building, but she turned. Mr Hyman was disappearing through the door with a big plastic bag over his shoulder. A fireman's lift. He was in the wrong job. The boot of his car was left open like a gaping mouth, a loose anus, it looked obscene and deserted.

'Let's wait.' That was Sydney.

'Let's get out of the car.' That was her. Mike was here now, she couldn't sit in the car and wait as if nothing had happened.

They stood on the concrete path in between the car and the small building and watched a man in a blue all-in-one suit tending to the boiler, a huge silvery monster, which looked as if it were new. Something must have gone really wrong for him to be here on Christmas Day. He waved cheerily. She found herself wishing she was perched high on the side of that great huge thing, a shiny precipice, looking after it, thinking about it, outside in the air.

She turned away. She couldn't smile or wave. She was in front of the plain brick building. It was so ordinary and yet so strange. She had not thought about mortuaries before, what they look like or what happens inside them. She looked up again at the Hebrew. Gold on stone, the only indication of something precious. A terrible pain hit her stomach. She realised that at her own death she would be on the other side. The Gentile side. She would not be with Mike. Why had they never thought of this and planned something different? They could have been together. She wanted him desperately.

As they approached, a young man with a soft face came out of the building. He was smartly dressed and clean.

'I've been told to come and warn you that there are other bodies in there too. There are three, OK?' He smiled as he spoke.

She stared at him wide-eyed. Surely they aren't talking about Mike, my lover, my friend for life? Bodies? These damned men are looking after him. No! She wanted to protest, to reclaim him, at the same time so scared to even see him.

She took a deep breath. Who are these strangers? They are Jewish and so is he. They would, she knew they would, look after him, clean him gently, carefully, with love, before they wrapped him up in a sweet white sheet. Then she remembered the plastic bag and the fireman's lift. She was wrong. They thought nothing of it. A ritual, he'd called it. We have to perform a ritual. What the hell do they do? Thank God she wouldn't be there for that. She didn't even need to know.

Mr Hyman stepped out blinking into the light.

'We're ready for you now.' They entered the building straight into a narrow corridor which turned immediately left and then right. She clutched the present, holding the flap of her coat over it at the front. She was walking forward but her body resisted. She didn't want to get there. There was a turning in the corridor. She saw a very small room on the left; there were some men there. They were dressed in long white coats and she had the impression they were washing their hands. They smiled at her; she looked away. She should never have had to see them. She didn't want to see or know any trace of what they did.

Sydney went in first and helped her over the threshold. She did go cold. The room was cold, refrigerated, but not only that, there was a deep shock of cold from within. The air was heady and sweet, sickly sweet. It arranged itself thickly inside her nostrils. She found it hard to walk. There were three long thin tables. She noticed with surprise that they were marble. Mike was lying asleep on a marble bed, covered in sheets. Three bodies! They were humps under white sheeting. They looked surprisingly small. Two were bodies and one was Mike. Mr Hyman moved to the head of the central bed. She had to negotiate. She needed to be near the middle bed without going too close to either of the others. Dead strangers. The beds were close together. She sidled up, the presence of what was behind her as insistent as what she was about to see.

'It's this one.' Her eyes darted wildly. 'Is she okay?' Mr Hyman asked.

'Yes,' she whined. 'Yes, I'm ready, I am. I'm frightened.' The last little admission escaped as he rolled back the sheet, carefully so it rested under the chin and still covered the ears. She supposed that any of the holes might let juices out. Life juices. And they wouldn't want you to see that. Mr Hyman hovered round the head, watching her carefully, his proximity telling them it really was a very silly thing for a young woman to be doing.

'We'll be all right,' she said, her voice high and thin.

'You'll have to be quick. Otherwise it'll make the whole thing late.' Mr Hyman seemed reluctant to leave and hovered for a second by the door, but she hadn't even heard.

It was as the door closed that she had started screaming, her face upturned towards the ceiling. It tore from her throat over and over, harsh and ragged, getting louder and louder each time. Wild, wild women's wailing. Even at the time through the centre of her grief she felt akin to women from Russia, women from Iran, who wept and gnashed and longed unbearably for their loved ones back. Women from everywhere.

The noise she made reminded her of when Sarah was born. The fierce pushing, pain and pleasure so peculiarly mixed together. The midwife had said time and again she could see the head, dark brown, wet hair. She had reached down and felt the shape, surprised by the hardness yet softness of its contours. She had let her fingertips brush it, but so lightly in case she should damage it, and then it retreated back, unsure, maybe stubborn.

Finally the head came out, the whole of her body stretched to its limits around this massive globe of bone. That moment imprinted on her mind, like a still photograph that will never fade. She had loved that head so strangely stuck between her legs, a moment that must have been quickly over but seemed to go on for ever. Whilst it lay there, nestling into the tops of her thighs, her bottom lying in the puddle that had come with it. She had screamed and screamed.

At the birth she hadn't realised that the midwife was calling her. 'Jane, Jane,' and then shouting, '*Stop screaming*, you don't need to.' She had stopped. The quiet was a shock. The peace was a shock. The light was dim. The screaming was from a past fear of what it might have been like, rather than to do with what was happening now. It was such a short moment really. A beautiful moment in amongst so many others, the memory tainted with regret that she had almost spoilt it by the noise.

Mike had been there, hovering around her head, wanting to relieve her, offer her comfort. He had stayed for the full eighteen hours, only leaving once for ten minutes to get a sandwich. When the baby was born he had held her for two hours and smiled. A lovely smile, so happy. Then he had fallen asleep in the chair and the nurse had come and put the baby back in the crib. But she had wanted something from him, urgently. It was something intangible. While he slept in the chair she had lain in bed, her mind racing, feeling sore and deeply disappointed. Much later, she realised she had wanted him to be the same as her, in the suffering and the delight. She had wanted him to give birth with her, so that he could really understand. He had disappointed her by being a man.

The pain of this memory was too much. Mike was gone. She strained against it, not wanting it to be, a bit of her believing she could prevent it. She wanted to see him, she needed to see him so badly, he would have to be alive. For her.

Her screaming was the same at the birth and now at death. But everything else was different. A lone, awful cry from before civilisation, that surprised her. Dimly she was aware of some shame, that she should be alone making a noise like this, an animal noise. She was pleased that only her father-in-law heard it. Sydney didn't talk much, he would keep it to himself. He would always know how she had felt.

Then suddenly he had put his arm across the top of her shoulders. She could remember the weight of his whole arm. It was heavy. He didn't hug her or pull her towards him, he only made the screaming stop, and then she saw the face.

'It's not Mike. It's definitely not him.' She sobbed like a child from the depths of her being. 'This isn't him, he didn't look like that.'

'No, he didn't look like that. He looks like that because he's dead.'

She rocked forwards and backwards, inclining her head this way and that, as if she thought a different angle would help, she would be able to know that it was him from the other side of the table.

'Where is his mouth? What have they done to his mouth? Where is his lip?' His bottom lip that used to be so curvaceous. Sarah took after him, had the same mouth. It had been his strongest point.

'They've tucked the bottom one under the top one. It's still there, it's to stop his mouth lolling open. That would be worse.' Yes, she thought, that would be worse. It would be nice just to see his whole face, instead of it looking so peculiar like that. Wouldn't you have thought they would have designed some small plastic contraption which unseen would keep the mouth closed? She thought of trussed chickens, and these other two people one behind her and one the other side. Were their top lips tucked away too?

She saw his wiry moustache. He did have a moustache, mostly browns and a few flecks of white. He had been getting older. He was forty-one. The moustache was different, sparse. A few thin wiry hairs licking around his top lip; even the hairs looked dead, as if they had been stuck back on one by one, at slightly odd angles.

Nothing looked right. The nose, normally big, bulbous and friendly, looked swollen, lopsided, encrusted with blood. His eyes deep crevices; little formless eyelashes, stuck together. His face sagged unfamiliarly, and yet the skin looked tight, thick, yellow. His top lip, that was his, yes definitely, large Cupid's bow, generous lip, she had loved the shape of it. That was there. It must be him. It was him, she knew it was. But it didn't look like him.

'Do you want to kiss him?'

How could he even ask? She had wanted to kiss him before they came in. But she couldn't kiss that face. It was far too cold. But suddenly without wanting to she found herself bending over that face and placing her lips firmly on Mike's cheek. She wanted to kiss him so badly, wanted him so badly, and here was this face. But it was cold. It wasn't him.

'They've broken his face. Sydney, they've broken his face.' She wasn't sure if it had been the hospital or something to do with these men. He had been badly hurt by someone, that was why he looked so awful. They'd broken his damned sweet face so that you couldn't tell it was him. It looked like they had made a deep, painful crevice in his cheek. It was concave.

Sydney hurried round. 'No they haven't, it's only because his muscles aren't working that the shape of his face is different. It's not broken. Really, it's not.'

'I'm not sure, I'm not sure. Poor Mike. I wish we could take him away with us. I don't like the men, I don't like the way they are looking after him.' She was pleading, sobbing, wanting. 'Jesus, I never knew it would be like *this*. I came to see Mike and it's awful, I didn't realise . . .' she had said Jesus. She had called him like people do. Why was that? Nobody came to help Jesus himself. He had been stuck on a cross and had died there. Could special things happen because it was his birthday? Could Mike come back? She was filled with the dawning realisation that no one was coming to put things right. This was also a new pain.

She looked at the face again. Peace and relief. They *were* his eyes. They were closed. The lids looked ordinary resting over the eyes underneath. They were the right shape and she knew they were his. He had those god-awful stubby eyelashes that were short and never curled. She liked them. They were his. It *is* him. She didn't really look at the rest of the sheeting, the mound of his chest, the points of his feet, or where his knees must be. In the back of her mind there were pictures with no words, of them taking away the sheet, his white flesh unheld by muscle, his penis retracted and small, and awful, awful marks, gashes hurriedly stuck together where the doctors had intruded desperately trying to keep him alive when there was no chance of it.

Her hands were clasped, knuckles just touching the marble in front, her head bowed. She was seeing through a blur of tears. She thought of the nativity, the shepherds bowing in prayer over the baby. The baby's body. Did Jesus have a nappy or did he soil the hay in the manger? It would be no good for the animals then. She was thinking of nonsense. It's just that it was Christmas Day, so she thought Jesus might have something to do with it. What was 'it'? Mike? The accident? She could make no sense. No sense of any of it.

'We'll have to go in a minute,' Sydney warned her. She looked up and saw tears running down his sagging cheeks. Just tears, no noise. She felt guilty. She had not thought about Sydney. He had lost his son. It was the wrong way round. You shouldn't see your son dead. Everything was wrong.

'I haven't given him his present.'

'What present?' Sydney did not understand.

'It's his Christmas present. I mean it's just a small present. It's nothing really. What will I do with it?' She held up the gawdy package. He was gone, but his present was still here. Awkwardly here.

Her mind worked fast. She would leave it secretly. There was no one to see. Who was Sydney to say she couldn't give her husband a present? She would tuck the book into his breast pocket and it wouldn't even show. It was only a slim volume. But then she remembered the marble slab and the sheet. It became painfully obvious to her in that instant that he had nothing on, no suit, no shirt, he was wrapped in a large piece of sheeting, that was it.

Her hand moved towards the sheet as if she planned to lift it and slip the book underneath. 'No! You can't do that,' Sydney shouted at her. The dullness lifted from his eyes, for a moment they sparkled with rage. 'Mike was a Jew. In Jewish law we come to this world with nothing and we leave it with nothing. That's what it says.'

She nodded her head up and down as if she was slowly understanding. We come with nothing and we leave with nothing. She looked again at the face of her husband. She couldn't squeeze any more out of it. It lay there like that whether she was here or not. Christmas Day or Midsummer Day, it made no difference. She would leave the room and it would still be there. She wouldn't be allowed back in. Should she go, or look again one last time? She looked again and it was just the same. He had already left.

On the way to the cemetery she threw the book out of the car window. She threw it to the wind. She thought someone might pick it up and think it was a lost Christmas present.

Where Will He Go?

Caroline Hallett

Being little I relied on Marie to tell me when something important had happened. In all things I was her disciple. I inherited her pyjamas, her black gym pumps, most of her thoughts and her old hairbands. I believed we were the same person, accidentally divided.

'Come!' she would shout 'Come! Quick! Quick! He's been. He's been again!' I always went when she called out.

I used to imagine that we shared the same bed because I sometimes fell asleep in her arms. Now I'm sure we didn't, we had our own beds. I know that now. If I crept into her bed at night they would come in the dark and carry me back to my own. I don't know who it was. Our mother, or some white swans with featherbed wings as I sometimes dreamed.

My own bed felt empty beneath the heavy blankets. If I lay too long alone, my hand would start to fidget and before I could help myself it would be picking holes in the wallpaper. They found those holes when they moved the bed one year. I've always had to pick at things, especially scabs.

In summer crane-flies would dizzy for hours round the dim room, waiting for dark so they could stagger across my face.

In winter the room was stiff and choked with cold. We dressed for bed in winceyette pyjamas, woollen bedjackets, bedsocks, dressing gowns. Hot-water bottles in woollen suits waited in our beds like tiny plump bodies. We kicked them to our feet and clenched them all night between bony ankles.

It was the days before electric blankets which could set beds alight if improperly used. We had no fire in our room, neither gas nor electric. Our mother was fearful of deadly fumes.

We slept in the room near Mother's under the eaves, Marie by the window and I close to the wall. She always woke first with the cold.

That year it had been mild; then the cold broke like the Deluge. The morning before Christmas Eve Marie woke me. 'Come! Quick!' she shouted. 'He's been. At last! At long last!'

I jumped out of bed, hoisting Marie's old winceyettes up at the knees, and padded across to her bed.

'Who?'

'Quick! Get into bed! He's been!'

I climbed in beside her.

'Who? Tell me!' I never knew. How could I know, it was always changing? I tried to remember the last time. The Giant again or the Prince? Wolf, Jack Frost, Dragon, Father Christmas, our own father even? Our father was coming home for Christmas; we didn't know quite when. Our mother said, 'Whenever he can get away.' It was one of the phrases that became attached to my father-in-my-mind. 'His work takes him abroad' was another and 'War-wounded'. I couldn't remember what he looked like, but I sometimes dreamed of a gigantic man, running yet barely moving, across the vast desolate space of Abroad. I couldn't see what was chasing him, but he was running, running to get away. His giant's work-clothes were rags that flew behind him in the wind and beneath them was his war-wound.

'Who?' said Marie loudly. 'Why are you so dumb? Do you have to be so dumb?'

'I don't think I am so dumb.'

'Silly! You're not meant to answer, I'm just telling you. Breathe out. Like this!'

I huffed.

'What can you see?'

'Smoke,' I said. 'Dragon smoke.'

'There! That's the clue! Who breathes on windowpanes?'

'Dragon?'

'So dumb! I'll give you one more clue! He's made of ice!'

'Jack Frost?'

'You got it.'

Marie clapped me on the back and I lurched out of bed.

'Quick! Get back in. He may still be near!'

Then she let me lift the curtain and look at the morning, lovely with frost, the fern forests of ice on our window.

'Go get the pennies.'

'Not yet,' I said. 'Let me look some more.'

We leaned our chins on the windowsill till my throat ached and my stomach felt full with looking.

'Shall we do it now?'

'Uhuh.'

I ran for the dirty old pennies in the cupboard and we put them in our mouths, one each, as we'd been told never to. When they were hot and wet we pressed them into the ice forests and made perfect round eyeholes, through which we could see the Flat Roof below. It was glistening, white and desolate, like the great plain of Abroad. I was shivering although I didn't feel cold.

Marie's eyes grew wide. 'I bet there's icicles! Let's get some!'

'How?' I couldn't imagine.

She was already yanking at the handle of the casement window. Ice squeaked and groaned as she tore the window open and cold air pushed past us into the room.

'Give us a leg-up!' said Marie, as she tried to heave herself up on to the sill. Astounded, I tried to get my leg up towards the window.

'Stupid! Don't you know? Leg-up means my leg, not yours. Get your shoulder under my leg.' I teetered under her weight as she pulled herself on to the sill.

'Marie!' I said, suddenly alarmed. 'We'll be in trouble! Don't!' But Marie was already disappearing from view.

'Hold me!' she shrieked.

I grabbed at her wrists and pulled. But the mass of her had already fallen and my hands were suddenly sweaty and pointless, podgy manacles that she easily slipped. With horror and envy I watched her slow slither down the pitched tiles towards the gutter. I wondered what would become of her now. Three feet beneath lay the Flat Roof. I imagined it a thin icy crust through which she would plunge into our father's locked and empty study. I could hear the soft sound of her woollen bedjacket brushing the frosted tiles as she struggled to keep her balance. Her bedsocks rested for a moment in the valley of the gutter, then with a rending sound the gutter gave way and Marie was in a heap below. She didn't move and miraculously the Roof held. I began to cry.

'Don't you cry!' she snapped. 'It's me that slipped. Why didn't you hold me?'

'We'll be in touble! Look at the gutter!' I whimpered.

Marie got up and looked.

'I'll just shove it back. It's only a stupid gutter. No one'll notice.'

I saw at once that she was right. I leaned out of the window and watched her walk to the gable end. The roof showed no signs of giving way. I couldn't even see a crack, only dark patches in the frost where Marie's bedsocks had warmed it. I felt suddenly lonely and wished I'd gone with her. She lay down along the edge of the roof above the water butt and leaned over. She looked peaceful, as though sleeping. She brought back two perfect icicles.

They tasted of grit and of the wind that blew from the gravel pit. Marie made me take off my bedjacket and tie it to the window handle. She used it to haul herself up.

'It's a bit stretched,' she said when she untied it.

'It's only a stupid bedjacket,' I said, sucking my icicle.

'You might be in trouble!'

'Why me?' I asked.

'It's your bedjacket.'

I saw at once that she was right and I shoved it under my bed.

Our mother called out to us from her room. We were making too much noise and it was too early.

Marie threw her icicle out of the window. I hid mine under my pillow for later.

Marie said that we should dress beneath the bedclothes as the Giant would be watching.

'Is he always watching us?' I asked.

'No, not always. But he knows when we're getting dressed and he doesn't like to see that, so then he watches to make sure he can't see.'

The day was different from others. Marie and I decorated the tree, with our attention hovering around Mother. We could track her through the smell of spice and fresh laundry, and when she opened up our father's study we were suddenly there behind her as she turned round in surprise. The room was damp and still and seemed strangely brown, with too many shelves. Other parts of the house were red and white or primrose, never brown. Mother opened windows and brought in paraffin heaters. She banged the dust out of the old brown sofa. Marie and I decided the room was too sad. We should make a paperchain that would loop from end to end. It took too long and our tongues ran dry, so we stuck up some holly instead.

The afternoon dipped into boredom. We had got too excited with waiting and now no one was noticing us. Marie said she would have to give me a haircut as everyone was too busy to realise that it was getting in my eyes. I ran to fetch the scissors that Mother used to cut gristle. Marie began with hope and flair. The style was daringly short, maybe an eighth of an inch in parts. Mother cried when she saw me. She sat down suddenly like a flat tyre and cried. 'Her curls!' she cried. 'Gone! And Daddy coming home! What'll I do? There's nothing, nothing I can do. God help me!' Marie was hiding somewhere. I tried singlehanded to comfort Mother. 'We can stick it back on,' I suggested, 'with flour and water.'

'I've no time, but I'll have to get you to Rene's somehow.'

Rene was the hairdresser down by the bus stop who did permanent waving and cuts and sets for the passengers. When Mother delivered me to her door with despair, Rene took me on herself. Her mouth went up at one side and down at the other.

'Oh my! Oh no!' She turned me round and round. She stuck her comb between her teeth and began to work.

'How . . . ?' She spoke through her comb, '. . . too late now . . . we'll just have to . . . not much we can do!'

'Do something, anything!' Mother pleaded.

Rene gave me a style all of my own, a crew-cut. I looked like a bottle-brush.

Marie was in disgrace. She developed a sudden illness with stomachache and scarlet cheeks. Mother gave her Bovril and stroked her hair and in a short while she was better, but we went to bed disappointed. Our father hadn't arrived. Maybe he wouldn't get away in time. Our mother said he had been held up, he might arrive any time. We were not reassured. I said I would have to sleep in Marie's bed in case he came back in the night and frightened us, and Mother didn't argue. She got eiderdowns from the attic and left them on the clothes-horse by the kitchen stove. She worried over the laundry, patting and smoothing the sheets down, picking at collars. We didn't know what to say to her. There was something that bothered me still. When we were in bed I asked Marie.

'Marie, where will he go when he comes? I mean in the night, where will he go?

Marie began with confidence. 'Well, if it is deep, deep in the night he may sleep on the sofa and not wake us.'

'But after that night, where will he go?'

'He may hide somewhere for us to find . . . the airing cupboard or somewhere . . .' Marie was faltering.

'But why?' I asked. She didn't answer.

I woke early, before Marie. I needed to pee badly. I hung on and on. I didn't like to go downstairs on my own and it was barely light. I squeezed and squeezed with my legs till it felt better. Then it would come on again until I knew I had to go. I crept out of Marie's bed. The morning was dim grey and the stone floor of the bathroom chilling through my bedsocks. I wandered to the stove to warm my hands. The embers were still glowing. I noticed acrid ash on a saucer and the eiderdowns had gone from the clothes-horse. I picked up a fat brown stub, something like a giant's dog end, and then I knew he must be there.

I crept along the hall and stopped at the half-open door of his study. I could smell paraffin and something else that I didn't recognise. With a shock I saw there was a body on the brown sofa, huddled beneath the eiderdowns. At first I thought it was dead. Then I heard the rasp of sleeping breath. I went up close. He wasn't so big at all. Even though I was little I could see that he was really quite small and fitted easily on the sofa. His face was wide and fleshy, with a surprisingly sharp nose. My heart was racing. Marie wasn't there to tell me what to do and I felt myself slipping into her place. I grew suddenly bold. I lifted his eyelid, very gently with my thumb.

'Are you in there?' I whispered so as not to wake the house up.

He twitched and I jumped back afraid.

Then he opened his eyes and I could see that they were brown like my own and that they creased when he smiled.

'Hullo! Who are you?'

It occurred to me then that I could answer, 'Marie.' Would he know? Maybe he remembered before Marie and I were divided. But instead I answered 'I'm the little one!' as I usually did.

'Anna,' he said. 'But where are your curls?' His voice was gritty and quiet.

'Some are in the dustbin here and some in the dustbin at Rene's.' I replied.

'I see.'

I felt suddenly cold in this brown room and I asked him, 'Can I get under the cover?'

It was as easy as climbing into Marie's bed, or Mother's, but once there I wondered if I had made a mistake. The eiderdowns smelt musty, and the other strong smell that was him filled my nose. He was shaking his head and looking at me with wet eyes. I tried to think of something to say.

'How is your wound?' I asked at last.

'My wound?'

'Your war-wound.'

'You mean my leg? Did you remember my leg?'

I didn't know how to answer.

'You've forgotten my peg! You used to play with it when you were learning to walk.'

'I forgot,' I said, relieved that my forgetting could be attached to something as minor as a leg. He seemed not to notice that I had forgotten him entirely.

'Look in the corner, over there.' I saw now, of course. I wasn't so surprised. Maybe I'd always known it.

'Don't you take the sock off at night?' I asked.

'Only occasionally,' he said, and he ran his stubby hand across my bristling head.

'I'm very sleepy,' he said and his dark eyes began to close and disappeared into their fleshy lids.

While he slept I took careful measurements of his face and head so that Marie would be able to tell me whether he was in fact gigantic or dwarfish. His forehead was wider than I could stretch.

'Marie!' I whispered into her hair. 'Come! Quick! He's here!'

I took her to where he was sleeping. She was sleepy and strangely quiet.

'Look, Marie! That's his wound' I said, pointing to the leg in the corner.

'That's not a wound!' said Marie, 'that's a leg.'

'It's his wound. He told me all about it and how he got away.' I lied. Marie believed me. She didn't think me capable of lying.

The long day began and Marie and I forgot to dress beneath the bedclothes.

We crept through the light-filled rooms fearful of waking him, wondering if we had dreamed him. Then he woke and began to click and clatter through the house, marking the space with the arc of his great limp. He sat in the armchair and watched us with big wet eyes. Marie and I drew closer to him until we sat playing close to his feet, and every few minutes he would stir, and lean forward to touch our heads.

Later Mother took him to the shops and left us with a babysitter, May, who was nearly a woman and born before the war.

'They need time to talk,' May explained blandly.

'Isn't the time here any good?' I asked.

'It's not the same.'

Marie was disgusted at being treated so shabbily and said so loudly all afternoon.

We went to bed early and we each draped one of Mother's crêpe stockings at the end of our bed.

Marie woke first as usual.

'Come! Quick! Let's see!' And she led me down to the brown room. The sofa was empty and the cold from the roof had re-entered during the night.

We couldn't speak. Why had he come and gone like that? Why had he cheated us? We wandered from room to room, listening at cupboard doors, then went upstairs slowly and waited outside Mother's room. The door was ajar and we pushed it open. Her breathing was different, heavier, and her body strangely humped. I knew from Marie that we shouldn't wake her. She slapped me gently on the arm and pointed to the floor under the bed.

'Look!' she whispered. Of course. The leg was lying neatly in the shadow at the end of the bed. He had been there all the time. I could see two heads now, and his sharp nose sticking into the air. Their bodies seemed joined in some way, so that I could no longer tell which was Mother and which him. I thought suddenly that maybe Marie and I had been joined like that, before we were accidentally divided. And then I knew that it is painful to be divided after being so much part of someone.

Marie was on her hands and knees beside the bed.

'Come! Touch it, I dare you. Touch his wound!'

'No, you!'

The leg was quite perfect, smooth and beige with a smart black sock and shiny shoe, and metal gleaming at the knee.

I pushed Marie forward and she touched it with her hand and started to laugh, holding in the sound. She took my hand and made me touch it too. We began to shake with laughing. It was spilling out of us and we couldn't stop it.

Mother opened her eyes and smiled. Then he turned over and looked at us.

'Well? Has he been? Did he come? What did he bring?'

Marie looked at me. We had both forgotten.

Still laughing we ran back to our room and found the beige crêpe stockings, stuffed and lumpy, lying at the foot of our beds.

The Woman Who Wanted to Miss Christmas

Jay Merill

Now the fluffy time snow and the snuffy puffy santa claus face with black printed bells, embossed holly all everywhere mistletoe, baubles right down to the advertisements in the newspaper. Affluent face, fat face, read me, buy me, how it all goes on. Buy my fat smiles for comfort it's good, cheer, so much so of the white christmas me, ideal. Make you happy, I am the smile in the paper, I am the smile in the thing you buy for happiness the same, oh with the wicked beard, for the children love the old man hot air cheeks in the winter cold and the ideal white of the icons, and kiss me quickly now that it's christmas for it's a different life when you're in the thick heart of it, and learning to live through somebody's other smile, end all deathened clouds of fluff fleecy as a dream but with money in the bank solidity pleasing to all the proper ones, everything, transparent as snow and yes more pure, and there was once a woman, home making, cake baking, one of that type, but still she did want, she felt she wanted, to miss it all but how, when she knew it was there she could not help knowing it was there and all about it. Did she want to resist it? Did she want to go against the grains of white and all the tinsel? Snowflakes, such melting sighs and also heavy words packed in all there like a mother's smile, and she, being a mother, if she had wanted to miss it could she have missed it and a similar thing with resistance, never nothing in a snowflake in all the states of it, always at least the one question and a suggestion of water. 'Do it for me-for-them, it's not much to ask for you to be happy to be happy to make them happy is it much?', and no, it wasn't as she could actually see, normal not even acquiescence is the matter as it's so very little as it is. She was allowed to choose important things they said for she was an adult, nevertheless a spoilsport and moreover she must be able to see that snowflakes were delightful. It did seem funny she could choose a big thing but not a little thing, and he-they saying yes it was, she was powerful and that was a big thing and this the christmas issue it was so small too small for her to notice and unworthy and the thing was normal and not even anything.

They were standing in this doorway and there was glitter on the glass above it, it coming up fast to christmas, and all you could hear the murmur of voices in the shiplike space beyond the door and she was frightened to wonder about the difference between a big and a little thing but now she could not stop doing it. The door opened and the noise was loud. She could not move her feet to go inside although they ached to move and it was because of the wondering, she also feared the knowledge of how easy it would be to go inside the door.

Outside were the little worlds in windows where toy animals moved arms stiffly, look she's sweeping the winter snow. Fur paws, she's sweeping the snow, she's going to sweep the snow, she's pretending to sweep the snow, they are pretending that she is seriously going to sweep the snow, she will always be sweeping the snow or she or they will be pretending she always will be till the world ends or the fur fabric paw is dismantled, and there's another little bear with a spade digging into the fluff and there's a cloud, a puff for parents the good ones hoping to hear children gasp. 'Look at the furry bear, the funny bear, do look at the little bear,' the parent-voices stiff with kindliness.

'Why won't you come in through the door and why won't you look at the windows? These things are only innocent,' the looks said.

But she had her way because he wanted to punish her. They went home on the bus and the children said, 'Why couldn't we go to see Father Christmas?'

He – wrapping the presents and writing, 'from mum and dad', on the labels and putting the presents by the christmas tree, wanting watching, and waiting for her to be watching and wanting not to be alone in this the good preparing of the presents; she knowing it was unreasonable to be unreasonable, frightened by the pain which was not well-defined and knowing it is easy to give in when a pain is not well-defined and the resistance is without foundation.

'What a fuss about nothing,' the man was thinking, and she, seeing the sulk of his lip. He was also secure in the knowledge of reasonableness of what was reasonable and of what one had a-every right to expect. She hated to know that the lip would smile up if she smiled down with a forgive-and-forget-twist to it.

Do you want to light the candles, dress the christmas tree, get out the twisted paper and chocolate money, and also, the small-sized, miniature-sized crackers with the purple and red and gold zigzags and those underneath in the box with the green and red and gold zigzags, five of each, ten to a box, have got to be tied to the branches, they must be spread out nicely-all-over the tree not bunched together. And don't put a purple and red and gold next to another purple and red and gold, put a green and red and gold alternately, it's better. And there should be something, cotton wool, put on top of the earth. You know very well what to do, you've done it before enough.

Things it would be unthinkable not to do them though not important.

'And because it isn't important you just might as well do it. Might as well as not, what is "not"?'

Awkward ways, he now no-energy eyes, bored, it's christmas tomorrow, but why won't she, so ridiculous but she'll soon be normal again though awkward she became normal again, when she'd got over it, he was busy, he had no time, she was obstinate, why was she being obstinate?

'You can be so absurd,' he said.

He – sitting in a sea of wrapping paper so busy, the gift

tags fluttered in the breath of his little accusation. She, standing in the hall because she had walked out into the hall and he, coming up to the door of the hall and saying, 'You're unreasonable.' He was facing her weary-not-wanting a row, he was not argumentative, he was busy and now this.

'Why don't you think of the children?'

He went back to the presents, there being many still to wrap, it was getting late, time was getting on, he wasn't going to get any help from *her* tonight but tomorrow probably surely she must be better by tomorrow. Arranging the presents into well-constructed groups with the big ones at the back so you could see all there was to see such a lot and in different wrapping papers with the reds and greens well mixed.

She – sitting on the bed, it's christmas tomorrow, properly christmas, the gorgeous day. Looking out at the sky, the dark, the hugeness of the sky, the heaviness of the dark and a few but not many stars. The sky-and-dark were big things and she looked out at them. She lifted her arms stiffly as if she were going to sweep the snow, she lifted her arm with intention, as if she were going to sweep the snow, she is pretending to sweep the snow, we are pretending that she is seriously going to sweep the snow and she-and-we look as if we always will be pretending that she always will be sweeping or will be about to sweep the snow. Till the world ends or she is dismantled, whichever is the sooner. She lowered her arm, and, although there was nothing inside her like a choosing of it, she began to laugh.

Daddy Christmas

Susan King

Angela snuggled down under her duvet. She could feel Mr Wilcox's present lying safely beside her. Sounds of Christmas music filtered upstairs from the television below. Any minute now her mum and dad would switch it off and come to bed. She'd been in bed for hours but she didn't feel in the least sleepy. In another half an hour, it would be Christmas Day and Daddy Christmas would be coming with her presents. She couldn't afford to drop off. Not now.

When she was very little, they had used Daddy Christmas as a bribe: 'Now Angela,' they'd say, 'if you're a good little girl, we'll ask Daddy Christmas to bring you a special present when he comes this year.' Or, more often, to threaten her: 'Angela, how could you get so filthy? You've been down in the cellar, haven't you? If you don't do as you're told, I'm going to tell Daddy Christmas not to come to visit you this Christmas at all.' Her dad, however, had never been able to hold the threat long; her tears were enough to make him relent and take her on to his lap. 'Come on, Marjorie,' he'd say, 'she didn't mean any harm.' Her dad had always stuck up for her. In his eyes she was perfect.

The Christmas music ended abruptly and Angela heard the sound of her mum opening the living-room door. 'I'll pull the plugs out and lock up,' she heard her dad say. 'Shall I bring you some hot chocolate?'

'No thanks, love. There's no need. I'll be asleep as soon as my head hits the pillow.'

'Well, I'll just tidy up a bit and then I'll be up.'

The door closed and she heard her mum's footsteps on the

stairs. She turned to Emily. 'I can't talk to you for a few minutes. Mum's coming.' Emily nodded and kept quiet. Angela heard the bedroom door open and felt the hall light fall on to her closed lids. Her mother crossed the room and her warm lips touched her forehead. She trembled in case her mother noticed the slight mound in the duvet made by Mr Wilcox's present. She wasn't worried about Emily; nobody could see Emily except herself. The door closed gently and her mother's footsteps moved away.

'It's all right,' she whispered to Emily. 'She didn't notice anything unusual.'

She hadn't been able to sleep that first Christmas either; that first time she'd seen Daddy Christmas for real. She wanted a bicycle, a blue and green one she'd seen in the shop window. She thought about it and thought about it until, in the end, she wrote to Daddy Christmas promising to be good for the rest of her life, if only he'd bring her the bicycle. Each time the letters arrived she searched for one from Lapland, but none came. Still she didn't give up hope. In bed she lay awake and watched the window for his sledge and listened for the sound of reindeer bells. None came. She closed her eyes. 'Please come,' she said, 'please.' And when she opened them, he was in the room.

She could hear her dad moving around downstairs, opening and closing doors, putting dishes into the sink, humming to himself. The light in her mum and dad's bedroom clicked off. She turned to Emily. 'It won't be long now,' she said.

'Will you be ready?' asked Emily

'Yes,' she said.

He'd been exactly as she'd expected him to be, that first time, but thinner. His red suit looked a size too big and his white beard covered almost all his face. He stood still for a moment and, convinced she was asleep, opened the bedroom door wide and pulled in a huge box. Her bicycle! She let out an,

'Oh!', and at once he stood up and looked at her. She held her breath and closed her eyes again. If he found out she was awake, he might be angry and take the bicycle away. She could smell him as he leaned over her. A damp smell she'd smelt somewhere else. She felt his hand touch her forehead and brush back her hair.

'Are you awake?' he said in a whisper. His beard tickled her face and she couldn't help twitching her nose. 'I think you are, aren't you? You're just pretending, you naughty little girl. Don't worry, Daddy Christmas isn't angry. He couldn't be angry with you. Not ever.'

He continued to stroke her hair and then she felt his breath on her face and then his mouth on hers, but it wasn't the sort of kiss her dad gave her. This was one was slobbery and lasted so long she thought she might stop breathing. She wanted him to stop and go away so she could look at her bicycle, but she thought that would be rude. After all, he was famous.

At last he finished, and she couldn't help wiping her mouth. It was sticky. She waited for him to say goodbye and disappear off to the other waiting boys and girls. Instead he had lifted the duvet cover and climbed in next to her.

Emily signalled her to be quiet. It was her dad coming upstairs. He stopped by her door for a moment before moving on. A series of noises followed each other: the click of the bathroom light, water running, a bedroom door opening.

Quiet for a few minutes and then her mother's voice through the bedroom wall. 'Barry, please don't. Not now. I'm tired.'

'Sorry, love. I just thought . . . it being Christmas and all.'

'Barry, really. Goodnight.'

'Goodnight, love.'

Silence.

She hadn't known what to do. Scream out for Dad? But Daddy Christmas was with her, and Daddy Christmas didn't do little girls any harm. All the story books said so.

Daddy Christmas started stroking her and whispering in her ear. 'We won't tell anyone. It'll be our secret. A special present for a little girl who's been so good.' His hand pulled up her nightie and touched her wee-wee. It was so hot it felt as if it was burning her.

'You like it, don't you, when Daddy Christmas holds you, like this?'

His hand squeezed hard and she felt something inside her. It felt like a finger.

'There, that doesn't hurt, does it?' She nodded. It didn't, but it felt strange. She felt strange. She'd never read anything about this in her storybooks. She plucked up courage to speak.

'What are you doing?

'Daddy Christmas is being nice, he's always nice to special little girls.' He was breathing very quickly now, and through the white whiskers his bright eyes stared at her. 'Daddy Christmas needs you. He thinks about you all year, your skin, your hair. He needs to touch them, to touch all of you. All of you.'

He climbed on top of her and the damp smell was in her lungs. He was struggling with his trousers and then something hard pushed between her legs. It was trying to get inside her. She didn't feel strange any more, she felt afraid. Afraid of Daddy Christmas: his voice whispering to her, this thing between her legs. She had to stop it. She pushed at Daddy Christmas. 'Stop it, stop it,' she screamed, but her screams were buried in the cloth of his jacket. She felt it tearing into her, pain searing through her body and then wetness soaking through and out of her, and into the sheet underneath.

She turned and looked at Emily's freckled face. She was the only person she'd ever told. She couldn't tell her mum, or anyone, not after what Daddy Christmas said. She couldn't understand why he'd hurt her. She kept crying, all the time he was cleaning her up, wiping her legs and bottom with the soft white flannel. She watched the water in the bowl turn as red as his jacket as he squeezed it out. Her tears fell into the water, making ripples on the surface.

'Now stop crying and be a big girl,' he said. 'Daddy Christmas didn't want to hurt you, but sometimes it happens that way. And you must never, never tell anyone, ever. It's our special secret. If you do, the police will come and take your mummy and daddy away, and you'll never see them again. Do you understand?'

She nodded and let him put a clean nightie on her. She didn't understand anything really, but she wanted to go to sleep so the pain would go away. Daddy Christmas tucked her in and said goodnight. 'Tomorrow, when you wake, it will be Christmas and you'll have your present to open,' he said before he disappeared.

She never rode her bicycle, ever. In the end her mum took it back to the shop 'I'll never understand you, Angela,' she said.

The next Christmas Angela didn't write to Daddy Christmas at all. If she didn't write, he wouldn't come. She was sure. She spent Christmas Eve decorating the Christmas tree with her mum. It was a large tree, much bigger than herself. She was decorating the lower branches, whilst her mum did the ones she couldn't reach. Coloured balls, chocolate shapes wrapped in silver paper and gold tinsel littered the floor.

'We must get some new decorations next year. These are getting too damp from that cellar. This one's mouldy,' her mum said, throwing a greenish reindeer into the bin.

Angela wasn't listening; she was taking her work very seriously. She chose a red ball and then a chocolate shape, a green ball, a chocolate shape, a silver ball . . . The next shape she pulled out was a figure in red and white, a Father Christmas. As she held it in her hand the memory of the previous Christmas came back to her, the smell, the pain and the blood. She looked at her mum, fixing the fairy on to the top of the tree. She could just ask.

'Mum, do you think Daddy Christmas will come to see me this year?'

'Well, after your ungrateful behaviour last Christmas, I shouldn't be surprised if he doesn't,' her mum answered from behind the Christmas tree. Angela took a deep breath. She wouldn't have to tell her mum everything.

'I don't think I want him to,' she said quietly. 'Will you tell him not to come.' Her mum came round from the other side of the tree.

'Why?'

'Because . . .'

'Oh, Angela, look at the mess you've made. You make me so cross sometimes. Go and get yourself cleaned up, or you won't get any presents at all.'

Angela looked down at her hand. She'd squeezed the chocolate Father Christmas so hard it had melted and dripped on to her clean dress.

'But, Mum . . .'

'Angela, I won't tell you again.'

'You won't forget to tell him, will you?' she said on her way out the door. Her mum didn't answer. She was wrapping tinsel around the tree.

All evening Angela watched her mum to see if she made any phone calls. It would be too late to write now. Once or twice the phone rang and her dad answered it, but her mum never went near the phone all evening. Perhaps he'd already left anyway. Lying in her darkened room, she kept her eyes focused on the door. She wouldn't close them once, she wouldn't even blink. She yawned and rubbed her eyes. She felt them close against her will. Just for a moment.

When she opened them again, he was in bed next to her. She could smell the dampness of his suit and saw the green tinge on his beard. She opened her mouth to cry out, but he put a hand over it. 'Don't scream, little angel,' he said. 'I won't hurt you this time.'

Daddy Christmas was a liar. It had hurt. She cried tears of hate into her pillow. Why had he picked her? She threw the doll he had given her when he'd finished out of the bed and heard it smash on to the floor. The movement made her gasp. She felt so sore and lonely. She wanted to die.

The door slowly opened again. Daddy Christmas was coming back! She felt herself slip down under the duvet, but no Daddy Christmas walked through the door. Instead, a girl of her own age, ginger hair and freckled face, came and sat on the bed. 'Who are you?'

'I'm Emily. I heard you crying. I've come to be your friend.'

Emily had been her friend over the next two years. She had needed her more and more as Daddy Christmas began to visit her more often, not just on Christmas Eve. After each visit, Emily would appear to comfort her. She would be there when Angela woke in the night unable to breathe, the bed soaked in sweat. She would turn up in the classroom the evenings Mr Tomkinson made her stay behind to resit whichever test she'd failed that week. She was there when the policeman came to the school to talk about road safety and Angela fainted. But she was never there when Daddy Christmas came. Then she was always alone.

It was Emily's idea to go to Leslie Wilcox. She didn't want to; Leslie Wilcox wasn't quite right in the head. Everyone knew that. He'd never been the same since his wife and daughter, Sally, had been killed crossing the road. He'd seen it happen, in front of his house. He'd hand-made the coffins himself, in three days. When Angela had watched the black car with the tiny coffin go past her house, she had wished she was the one lying in the polished box under the flowers. Her dad had put his arm around her and pulled her away from the window. 'Come away, love,' he'd said. 'Don't let it upset you.'

When he had opened the door, she wanted to run away. He was only the same age as her dad, but he looked older, his uncombed hair streaked with grey and lines around his dull, staring eyes. His clothes were stained and dirty, and he smelt of the toilet. 'I've brought you these,' she said, holding out the tiny bunch of buttercups and daisies. Like everyone else, he didn't see Emily standing beside her.

After a few visits he began to call her Sally, and Angela let him brush her hair, while she told him tales of school. Each time she arrived, he would be watching for her in the window. It wasn't long before Emily began to pester her. 'Ask him soon or he won't have time. It's only two months to Christmas.'

Angela moved her leg and felt her skin touch wood. He'd had plenty of time. He'd made her a beautiful present: a work of art. Everyone said he was funny in the head but still marvellous with his hands. He hadn't wondered at the strangeness of her request, he would have given her anything she asked for. This was all she needed.

'He's coming,' Emily said. 'I can hear him.'

Angela could hear her heart pounding. 'Are you going to stay?'

'Of course. I wouldn't miss it for the world.'

The door handle turned and slowly the door opened to admit the red-suited figure she knew so well. She wasn't frightened now. Her hand took hold of the handle and pulled back the bow. The figure closed the door and turned to face her. 'It's Daddy Christmas,' it said. 'Have you been a good girl?'

She threw back the duvet, lifted the crossbow and fired. She heard a thud and watched him jerk backwards. He hung on to the back of the door like a rag doll pinned by a dart. Around the arrow, his suit turned redder and a trickle of blood ran down the white beard, reminding Angela of raspberry ripple ice-cream. She let the crossbow fall on to her lap.

'Good shot,' said Emily.

'Not bad,' said Angela. 'I suppose I'd better go and tell Mum and Dad. I don't know what they're going to say.'

First Kiss

Jenny Palmer

I met him at the end-of-term Christmas dance. It was the first opportunity for romance I'd had. I was now in the sixth form and still hadn't had a 'relationship' of any sort. Everyone else talked avidly about their boyfriends. I hadn't been anywhere socially, except to the village socials twice a year and to the Mecca on Boxing Day. It had become the highlight of the year. On these nights we persuaded my brother to give us a lift home. Otherwise the last bus home was at eight o'clock, and there was very little you could do before eight, not even go to the cinema.

This night I was determined something should happen. Jack had asked me for a dance and then he'd hung around and wanted to chat. And there was something more than that. I knew it. I felt it. He was interested in me physically. Nothing else could explain why he hung around like that. I didn't know what sexual feelings were from first hand experience, but I'd heard so much about them from my class-mates that I couldn't mistake them. Now something was actually happening to me.

He wouldn't suspect I had never kissed a boy before. I would appear as if I knew everything. When he suggested we go into one of the classrooms, I followed him blindly. There were other couples standing around in clusters, snogging. I was determined to get in on the act.

He took hold of me around the waist and his lips came close to mine. Then he seized me with his lips. I tried not to register fright. Should I keep my eyes open or shut? I had not been schooled in this. I kept them open the whole time to be sure of not missing anything. When he stuck his tongue in my mouth, I thought I would die of suffocation. No one had prepared me for this. You didn't see it in the movies. I was shocked. I was excited. I went rigid, stifling any feelings.

'Have you never done French kissing before?' he asked.

'Oh. It's not that,' I said, flustered. I was good at bluffing. I didn't let on that I had done no kissing before of any sort. Not even with my mother.

He took my embarrassment for passion and continued with the kissing. We kept it up for some time and then we heard them call the last dance. It would be a slow one. I'd often watched from the sidelines in the village socials as couples clung to each other, as if they'd never see each other again. I'd observed carefully the girls putting their hands round the boys' necks, to show affection. I was eager to try it out. Now my turn had come. I was going to make the most of it. We danced cheek to cheek. I felt the stubble on his chin, and the smell of his aftershave. Brut for men. It was all the rage at the time. It made me feel slightly giddy. But I didn't care.

Finally, I had a boyfriend.

'Want to meet next Saturday?' he suggested. 'I'll meet you from the bus.'

'Fine,' I said without thinking. And we kissed goodnight.

It wasn't until I got home that night that I remembered the problem of transport. I would have to prevail upon somebody at home to take me to the bus in the next village. How was I going to organise it? I racked my brains.

I could ask my dad outright, but I was too much of a coward for that. I didn't particularly want my brother to know I had a date, so I couldn't ask him. There was only one thing for it. I would have to prevail upon my mum to ask my dad to give me a lift to the nearest bus stop, two and a half miles away.

By the time the Saturday night came round I still hadn't had a definite answer. I'd mentioned it to my mum, but nothing had happened. At least she hadn't broached the subject again. By teatime I was almost in a frenzy. Who was going to take me? When my dad went out to the milking without anything being said, I finally demanded the answer from Mum.

'What did he say?'

'He can't take you,' she said. 'He's too busy.' Just like that. Matter of fact.

'You never even asked him,' I exploded. 'You don't want me to have a social life. That's what it is. I've been waiting for this night all week. It's all been fixed.'

I didn't tell her where I was going or who with. And she didn't ask.

I had borrowed a dress from my elder sister, a blue pinafore dress which had been very much in vogue the year before. I had the shoes, the perfume, everything. How could he be busy on a night like this? On my night out. It would only take him twenty minutes there and back. Jack was going to be meeting me in a couple of hours and nobody was going to take me to the bus.

'I'll walk to the bus.' I said. 'That's what I'll do.'

'You can't walk in this weather,' said my mother. 'It's two and a half miles. There's snow everywhere.'

'I don't care,' I said. 'There isn't time to go by the road so I'll go down the fields.'

'It's a foot deep down the bottoms,' she said. 'And it'll be pitch black. You can't go in this.'

I charged upstairs. I put on my dress and started making up my face.

'What are you doing?' said my younger sister.

'I'm going out,' I said.

Then I went back downstairs, put on my wellies, put my shoes in a bag and took a torch.

'And how will you get back?' asked my mother, as I was leaving the house. She had realised she couldn't stop me.

'I'll work that out later on,' I said. And before she could say any more I stormed out, through the gate at the bottom of the yard where my father was milking and into the fields.

The weather was bitter. But I determined not to feel the cold. It would be all right once I got started. I would hardly feel it then, at the speed I was going. I set off down the fields. In the distance I could see our hill, lit slightly by a thin moon.

It had a timeless sort of quality about it. How many years had it been there? Since the Ice Age, when it was said to have got its flat top. How many scenes had it witnessed in its time? Another one wouldn't go amiss. So often in summer we'd sketched it from the top of Big Field. We could do it by heart now, without having to look at it. I felt comforted, momentarily. But I was going to leave it tonight. Perhaps one day I would leave it for good.

There was a thin crescent moon in the sky, but it was hardly enough to show me the way. I didn't have time to be looking at the sky anyway. The ground was treacherous underfoot. One foot wrong and I could be up to my neck in a snowdrift.

Ten minutes later I'd reached the 'bottoms', which led out on to the road. It was here I hit the deep snow. I trudged through, the snow reaching up to the top of my wellingtons in places. The ground was a mass of white. It had an eerie quality about it. Anything could come at you in the dark. My mother had told me stories as a child about boggarts jumping out at naughty children and carrying them away. They lurked in hedgerows, waiting for their prey to come along, or sometimes they lurked in the 'other room' at night, when we didn't go to bed early enough. But I wasn't afraid of boggarts tonight. They wouldn't have stood much of a chance in the mood I was in. But why was I trudging through thick snow to meet a man I didn't know, and didn't even know if I liked? Was it all for the sake of a kiss?

As soon as I got through the deep bit, I was on to the road. The next couple of miles would be plain sailing. I knew the route well. All I had to do was keep up my pace and I would get there on time for the bus. When I reached the village three quarters of an hour later I was out of breath.

'Can I leave my wellies at the back of the shop?' I said to Mr Pinder. It was a habit we'd got into in the choir days, when we'd first started wearing stilettos. I didn't wear stilettos any more but I certainly wasn't going out in wellies on my first date. I would just have to pick them up on the way back. They would be safe. Nobody would steal a pair of wellingtons.

'Where are you off to tonight, then? Got a date?' said Mr Pinder, joking.

'Yes,' I said proudly. I wanted somebody to know about this. There wasn't much point otherwise.

By eight o'clock I was at the appointed place. Jack was waiting for me. He was standing outside a white MG.

So he had a car. Why hadn't he told me? Why hadn't I asked him? He could have picked me up from home and saved me all the trouble.

I was exhausted and the evening hadn't even started.

'There's a party on,' he said. 'Would you like to go?'

I had never been to a party, apart from friends' birthday parties. I didn't know what to expect. I had heard that they could be quite riotous events. I was game. I hadn't made all that effort for nothing. Besides, I was ready for a bit more of the kissing. The thoughts of the last one had lingered on long after the kiss had finished.

'I haven't got a lift back,' I explained.

'No problem,' he said. 'I'll run you back after.' I couldn't believe anything could be so easy.

I was in love with Jack already, even though I knew nothing about him. He had a car. He would run me home. What more could I want? Besides, he knew where to go and what to do. Parties and everything. And he knew about kissing.

It didn't take long to get to the party. We parked outside and walked in. I cast a glance around the hall. I didn't know a soul. But it was all a bit too familiar. I recognised the sort of event immediately. It was a village social, just like the ones we had at home. My heart sank. I was hoping for something a bit more exciting. Nothing riotous could happen here. It was a village hall.

We walked over to a group of girls. They were younger than me. I thought I recognised some of them from school. I said hello politely and then got Jack to dance with me. It was a Gay Gordons, I knew it well. Hadn't I had enough practice? I knew them all – waltz, foxtrot, quickstep, cha-cha-cha. I hadn't been to the dance classes for nothing. I managed to keep him on the dance floor for most of the evening.

'Let's have a drink,' said Jack at one point. I think he was feeling a bit tired. Suddenly somebody appeared with a camera.

'It's a Swinger,' he said. 'Develops immediately.'

I posed with Jack for the picture. He slid his arm round my waist and I tried to compose my face.

The man took the picture and then handed over the photo to Jack.

'Here, you have it,' he said. 'As a memento.'

'Why?' I said. But I took it.

I looked at the picture. It meant nothing to me. Just two people standing together at a dance. Later I would take it home. I would stick it in my photo album. Along with the other ones of me growing up. I would write 'Jack, 1965. First date' underneath. I would look at it, constantly trying to conjure up the feeling of the moment. But all there would be was this questioning expression on my face.

'What am I doing here?' it seemed to say. To all intents and purposes we could have been a couple, but somehow we weren't.

Jack brought me home that night and dropped me off at the top of the meadow, by the telephone box. We stayed together for a few minutes in the car to say goodnight. As he was kissing me goodnight, I suddenly remembered the wellies at the back of the shop but I wasn't going to mention them now. I would have to go and pick them up the next day.

'I'll ring you over the holidays,' he said, as he left.

I waited through Christmas Day and Boxing Day. Thoughts of that kiss lingered on in my mind. They got me through the hours of television, the gatherings of relations, and the tedium of school holidays when there was nothing to think about but going back to school in the New Year.

I eagerly awaited the phone call. Finally it came just before the New Year. He took me to the local pub to break the news.

'I think we ought to finish,' he said, out of the blue.

'Finish,' I said. I was speechless. We had only just got started.

I was expecting the relationship to go on indefinitely. Three weeks was hardly any time at all. Besides, there'd been Christmas when we'd hardly seen each other. Our relationship was being nipped in the bud, just as I was getting into my stride.

He was going out with a third-former now, he told me. It was someone he'd known all along.

'We can still be friends,' he told me.

'Like hell,' I thought.

My mind flashed back to the village social he had taken me to before Christmas. He had known that girl then. So had been two-timing, all along. It was the worst insult. He must have been fixing up a date that very night.

'See you,' I said, as he dropped me off at the top of the meadow. He would soon tire of her and want me back again.

I blanked him out of my mind after that. I felt a pang whenever I heard his name mentioned at school, but I didn't react.

'He's a flirt,' everybody told me. Secretly I missed my nights out. The ones I'd planned in my head.

'Perhaps it was because I wouldn't go all the way,' I thought. I had baulked at anything beyond kissing. Or maybe he was tired of the thought of picking me up from home and taking me back every time. We lived quite a way out.

It would have been very time-consuming. He could hardly
have got bored with me. There hadn't been time. The affair
had only lasted three weeks. And there had been Christmas
in the middle of it.

No Flowers – on Request

Petronella Breinburg

There was nothing wrong with insomnia, under such circumstances. At the same time a person can't help wanting to get some sleep, so Cheryl thought as she began counting sheep.

Soon she got to 500 sheep. True, she could have made mistakes in counting because once or twice she stopped, because she thought that someone had rung her door bell.

'It *is* the door bell,' thought Cheryl, and leapt out of bed. She took three or four rungs of the staircase at a time. She was sure that it was the police, but when she got to the front door and flung it open, all that hit her was a strong and very cold breeze.

'There *was* someone here.' She sniffed. 'Mm . . . strange, it's like scent, not perfume, more like lilac spray, the one Mum always used.'

Cheryl shrugged. On her way back upstairs she glanced with a sneer at the door leading to the flat downstairs. Once she and her mother occupied that ground-floor flat. But when a lone parent and her two young children needed accommodation, the Housing Association asked Cheryl and her mother to move upstairs. Her mother wasn't too keen. That was because her mother hadn't been too well. It was her kidneys, they told her. She had two very bad kidneys which might need removing. Also, her mother needed a special diet, besides rest.

'Stupid,' Cheryl thought again. The two things did not go together. Special diets needed extra money, and for extra money Mum had to slog her guts out for hours of overtime.

Rest? What's rest? If Mum wasn't in hospital she would have been working even on New Year's Day.

Cheryl got back to bed, but this time she was sure that she was not going to fall asleep. She was thinking, what if something went wrong after all? Then at once she rebuked herself. Don't be stupid, nothing will go wrong! Not now! Please God, not now, they said so at the hospital, that if anything was to go wrong, it would have done so by now. It would've happened on Thursday, which was the crucial day. Cheryl kept setting questions and answering them herself. At times she appeared to be convinced that her mother was not seriously ill in the local hospital, at other times she came near despair.

Cheryl shivered, not only due to the cold wind blowing in through the various cracks in the walls above the window. She also felt hungry. 'Wish there was something to eat. But if I eat that piece of bread now, I'll have to go without in the morning. Anyway, it will be morning soon, so stop grumbling!' she told her tummy.

Cheryl listened. What was that? Nah, it was only *them* downstairs! She listened again. Something was going on. True, the girl downstairs, being the 'entertaining' kind, often had male visitors at all hours. Often these male visitors had mistakenly rung the upstairs bell instead of the downstairs one. That ringing of the wrong bell often infuriated Cheryl and her mother. Cheryl had placed their family name in huge letters beside the bell, plus an arrow pointing upstairs. Yet the mistakes were still made; sometimes at two in the morning, sometimes four o'clock, they'd hear voices, or scuffles downstairs.

But what was going on at that very moment was not a scuffle. It was not as noisy as the usual fights. It was more like a sort of groan. 'Wonder if someone is ill?' thought Cheryl. For a moment she thought of going downstairs to knock. She was sure that she'd feel guilty for the rest of her life if someone was ill and she didn't help. What of the children? They were often left alone. That was after Cheryl's mother refused to keep them while their own mother went tramping round London's nightspots, Cheryl's mother had said.

'Wish Mum was here,' thought Cheryl sadly. 'She'd know what to do. Mind you, once she'd interfered and called the police, because the girl was screaming blue murder for help. But when the police came, what happened? Nothing! The girl hid herself and one of her men, the very one who was bashing her head in, told the police that the girl was out. Didn't Mum look stupid!'

Cheryl tried but failed not to keep thinking about her mother. 'Mum'll be fine, you can't keep Mum's head under water no matter how hard you try.' Mum was one of those people who would be dead and yet get up and walk. That is what happened that first night after her operation. With all those bottles and drips hanging from her side, and one from her arm, Mum had tried to get up. If that nurse had not been fully awake, my poor mum would have been dead by now, maybe. She would have got up and pulled that tube out of her side, the nurse had afterward said, and the blood would have come pouring out from that big hole the doctor had made in her side.

Cheryl got out of bed. 'Something *is* going on.' She went to listen by the staircase. 'There are more than two people downstairs!' Feeling ashamed for doing it, yet not being able to stop herself, Cheryl put her head down to the floor, where the noise came from. She listened. There were muffled voices. It was as if people were mumbling a chant.

Suddenly, fear got hold of Cheryl. 'Oh no, that girl is doing some sort of witchcraft! Oh, my God, the children! She's sacrificing one! There was that thing in the papers about some woman, some religious maniac, who sacrificed her son . . . bleedin' idiot. They should hang those women.'

Cheryl got off the floor and tiptoed to make sure the door to her apartment was locked.

The door chain was fastened, but Cheryl got that huge iron hammer her mother used to break coconuts. 'Anyone trying to come up here will get this right across his bleedin' head,' she thought, then crawled back to bed and pulled the sheets high over her head.

There seemed to be hours going by yet the chanting and moaning went on. The mumbling noise was louder than before. The people making it were right under Cheryl's bedroom now. She remembered her mother hating to give up that room. It was a nice room, and she could open the window in the morning and see the clock by the tower across the common. Also, she often said that she could hear the striking of the clock when it was very quiet, and this soothed her to sleep.

People were singing softly now – they were singing religious hymns. Was it imagination or did the front door get shut? Curiosity got hold of her again and Cheryl tiptoed to the sitting room. She daren't put the light on, and had only a faint streak of light from the street lamp. 'There could have been dozens of people there. Wish we hadn't gone and bought this carpet,' Cheryl thought. 'If it wasn't for this thick carpet, I'd probably find a crack in the floor to peep through,' Cheryl continued to think in a whisper.

A car pulled up outside. 'Shall I open the curtains just a tiny bit? Nah, stupid, they'll see you, and they usually put a curse on you if you see what they're doing. Don't be daft! You don't believe in that nonsense, do you? Only if you believe can they hurt you. Besides, it's your duty to see what happens so that if tomorrow one or both of those kids are missing, you can tell the police what you saw and heard. Now, be brave, count to three, then open just a bit of the curtains. One, two, three . . .' She pulled the curtain aside.

'Wait, it's a black car, and other cars, let me see, three cars, one behind the other. But this girl, she don't know people with long posh cars like those. Wait, there's something strange about that car in front, that longer one. Wait, wait, they're coming out. Oh God, they've killed the child, or both. That's a coffin, and a big one. That's not a child's coffin. They've got both kids in there. Quick, don't let them see you!'

Cheryl crouched quickly on the floor by the window. Her heart beat violently. She clasped her hand over her mouth, just in case a scream should try and get out involuntarily. But what if they knew that she was eavesdropping and peeping, she wondered?

'They know! I'm sure they know! They've got some extra power and know everything. Mum used to say that my granny used to have power to know things that happened when she wasn't there. No, I mustn't look again. Please God, don't let me look again.'

But Cheryl somehow couldn't stop herself raising her head to peep. It was as if she had to. Someone or something was forcing her to look. This time she felt her fingers opening the curtain, as if the fingers had a will of their own. She knew for certain that they knew she was there and wanted her to see them. They now had the coffin in the long black car. A man, dressed in a coat, got into the driver's seat. Other people got in their cars. There were all kinds of people, men and women, blacks and whites. At first, Cheryl could not make them out, then she saw one of her mother's friends, then another. 'Nah,' thought Cheryl. 'I'm wrong. They can't be Mum's friends.' The cars drove off and turned left up the hill and out of sight.

Cheryl felt strangely sick. Her vision became dim as if a cloud had come over the house. Just before she slid to the floor, Cheryl thought she heard her mother's voice saying, 'Don't cry, Cheryl. Please don't cry!'

A bright sunlight sending its rays through the window woke Cheryl up. She had overslept. Her body ached too. There were large marks along her arm because she had slept with the dressing-gown cord under her arm. 'But what am I doing here?' For a moment Cheryl had forgotten the scene of that early morning. When she did remember, a chill ran up her back. Again there were goose-pimples on her arm. She listened for any sound of children coming from downstairs, but there were none.

'I'll go down and knock. If she doesn't produce the kids, I'll phone the coppers at once,' she thought, while dressing and eating all at the same time.

Cheryl dressed, and was pleased that, it being New Year's weekend, she need not go to her Saturday job. She went downstairs and knocked, but she was out of luck. Either the young woman downstairs was asleep, dead or didn't want to answer.

Returning upstairs, Cheryl thought, 'How I wish Mum was here. She'd know what to do. What if I phone the cops, and they come, only to find the children well and happy? What if the whole thing was just a horrible dream, a nightmare?'

Somehow, the morning went. Since her mother had been admitted to the hospital, she spent lunch visiting her there. In the ward, Cheryl's mother's bed had been placed near the nurse's table.

'Why did they move you?' asked Cheryl.

'Oh, that,' laughed Cheryl's mother.

Cheryl's mother was a stocky woman who looked older than her real age because of hard work. Her hands were strong, though, and there was that look of determination on her face. A look which made her specialist say to Cheryl before the operation, 'It's a fifty – fifty chance of her coming through the operation. This is a big one, but she's a strong woman.'

'And what happened to all your flowers?' asked Cheryl.

Her mother's friends and colleagues at work had been sending what looked like tons of flowers, but now they were all gone.

'The smell of them, and they got little green flies,' explained Cheryl's mum.

'And she wants to get home to cook,' mocked a young nurse who just then came to give Cheryl's mum some tablets to swallow.

'She what?' asked Cheryl.

'She's been getting up at four o'clock in the morning to

go home,' supplied the patient in the bed next to Cheryl's mum's. 'Wants to be home for New Year's.'

'What on earth for?' laughed Cheryl. 'You're better off here, I can tell you that.'

There was just time for Cheryl to bid her mother goodbye, and run for the bus.

By afternoon, when the housework was finished, Cheryl was ready to drop. Yet she had to run back to her mother's hospital. So busy was Cheryl that she forgot all about the young woman downstairs and what she'd been up to with the kids. Not until she got home and saw the woman in the garden did she remember.

'Where're the kids?' asked Cheryl unceremoniously.

Cheryl had no time to stand and argue, but when the young woman said that the kids were at their gran's for the weekend, Cheryl burst out, 'You're a liar! I saw you last night, er . . . early this morning. You had some sort of ceremony. I saw it. I'll tell the police you've done something to your kids.'

'Me? I wasn't even here, I was at my mother's,' said the young woman.

She gave Cheryl a nasty look, dashed into her own flat and slammed the door. Cheryl heard her putting the chain in place.

'I'll tell!' Cheryl shouted through the letterbox.

Cheryl got to the phone, but unluckily for her there were two people waiting to use it. 'Besides,' she told herself, 'I have no proof. Maybe the young woman didn't actually kill the kids. But she did something all the same. But the police, knowing them, wouldn't be interested unless she actually harmed them. And the whole thing was some sort of mock funeral. Yes, everything like a funeral, except, er, flowers, no flowers!'

At the hospital, Cheryl had no chance to tell her mum. The place was full of visitors. Some of her mum's workmates were there too, with more flowers, and Mum looked very happy.

In any case, Cheryl did not stay for long. She went back

home. That night she waited to see if anything more would happen, but nothing did. Sunday came and Cheryl worked at her books, ready for her mock exam in the New Year. She cooked, visited her mother, came home. Her mother was getting better and looked very happy and relaxed, so Cheryl felt relieved, even hummed a tune.

Cheryl was a bit surprised when she came home and found the two children playing happily in the garden.

Cheryl badly wanted to go downstairs and apologise. But when she finally made herself go down and knock on the door downstairs, the young woman refused to open the door.

Late that afternoon Cheryl had to leave and take clean clothing back to the hospital, where they told her that her mother had made a remarkable recovery.

'Kept saying that she's ready to go home,' said a patient.

The nurse cleared her throat, and whatever the patient was going to say next didn't come. Instead, the patient began to talk to someone else. Cheryl and her mother made plans. Cheryl was to do well at school. She was not to worry. She'd pass her chemistry and all that she needed to go on the course. Even if she didn't get through this year, there were many more years. The main thing was that she must not give up. Try and try again. Then, to Cheryl's surprise, her mother kissed her. Her mother has never been the one to show emotions, but today she did. Cheryl was very happy and relieved. She knew that her mother was on the way to recovery. 'She looked so well,' she thought when she left the hospital.

That night Cheryl slept well. Then a banging at the door, together with a long ring at the door bell, woke her. At first she thought that she was dreaming again, because by then she was sure that she had dreamed that awful funeral scene, with its black hearse, cars and things. The poor young woman wasn't even home that weekend.

But the ringing continued, and then the young woman downstairs shouted her name. 'Cheryl! Cheryl!'

'It's not a dream,' said Cheryl, and got out of bed.

She reached the stairs, shouting, 'I'm coming, I'm coming! Don't break the door down!'

Cheryl opened the door to see the young woman downstairs staring at her. Behind her was a policewoman, then a policeman, one was a black woman and it was she who came up to speak to Cheryl.

'You Cheryl Moss?'

'Yes! But what have I done?' Cheryl asked, the way she always asked when the police came knocking at doors, which was often in the street she lived.

'Er,' said the policewoman. 'You're wanted at the hospital. We'll take you.'

'I'll go with her,' said the young woman downstairs. 'She can't go alone.' She got dressed and got in the police car to go to the hospital.

At the hospital, Cheryl was taken to her mother in a side room.

'Mum!' The word was a whisper. 'Oh, God, no!'

'Hold her! She's going to faint,' said the policeman.

'Mum, oh, Mum!'

The faces around Cheryl began to fade away, so did the voices. A long time seemed to pass before voices came back to Cheryl. 'Said she didn't want any tears.' Cheryl noticed a nurse, who was trying to make Cheryl drink something.

'My mother, Mother . . . wasn't a dream at all . . .'

'She said, kept complaining about money spent on flowers,' a voice said.

Cheryl kept saying, 'It wasn't a dream . . . it wasn't . . . I . . .'

'Here, drink this,' said a voice.

'Three days,' Cheryl whispered. 'In Guyana they believe in the three days in front thing . . .'

'What's that?' asked the nurse.

'Nothing.' Cheryl took a deep breath, held her head high, her back straight, her shoulders back; she gave a glance at her mother's peaceful face and walked into the fresh air.

The Name of a Very Good Man

Alison Campbell

Nancy had no memory of that time spent by the pillar box. She came to, as if out of a deep dream. The muscles of her arm and fingers particularly had been numb, then stiff, and she had felt very achy generally from standing still so long.

Droplets of snow had landed and melted, landed and melted, on the black woollen glove on her extended hand. The writing on the envelope between her fingers was slowly obliterated by four hours' worth of powdery snowflakes.

She came to as suddenly as she had frozen up, on that particular corridor of Byres Road where she had been about to post a card for Christmas – to her penfriend in Hamilton, New Zealand. She had no real knowledge of those four hours, or how they'd passed. Only faint fleeting images now and again. Or were they dreams?

She *did* dream recurrently of standing on the east coast, looking out across the expanse of cold grey North Sea to Norway. A ship was always caught in a glitter of winter sunshine on the horizon. It was supposed to be moving but somehow it never got any nearer to the coast.

Nancy felt the expanse of time she'd stood there at the pillar box was fuller, and at the same time emptier, than any dream.

Her great-nephew, in the days when he'd been brought to see her, had said, 'Auntie Nance, which is longer, miles or hours?'

She remembered explaining carefully that they were different and couldn't be compared.

Now, she wasn't so sure.

'See out there?'

The other girl glanced outside.

'What?'

'That woman,' the first girl said. 'Beside the pillar box. She hasn't moved for at least two hours. Not since I started this.' And she stuck the petite pink shovel into the barrel of pot-pourri she'd been bagging.

The second girl screwed up her eyes behind her glasses.

'She's certainly taking a long time posting her letter. She looks kind of . . . strange. D'you think she's okay?' She lifted the skewed cards from the revolving rack to re-sort them.

The first girl said, 'Maybe not. We'll tell Mrs Macgregor when she gets back from lunch.'

'Mrs Macgregor?'

'What is it, Fiona?'

Mrs Macgregor eased off her galoshes as she hung up her mackintosh and stepped into crimson high heels. She pulled down the waist of her mohair jumper and picked stray fluff from her skirt with long burgundy nails.

'Me and Molly were watching that woman out there. We think it's – I think it's weird. She's not moved since I started the pot-pourri this morning.'

Mrs Macgregor peered over the glass shelving in the front of the window. It was dark already – she must have had a longer lunch hour with Jimmy than she'd realised – but she could see the woman clearly enough.

'She's been like that for hours, hasn't she, Molly?'

'Ah-ha, hours, Mrs Macgregor.'

'Okay, girls.' Mrs Macgregor glanced at her watch. The tiny mascots on the adjacent gold chain tinkled, a sotto version of the bamboo-and-shell wind chimes by the shop door. She patted Fiona back to the knot of customers at the till.

'If nothing's happened by 4.30, I'll see about it.'

It was as if Nancy was in some deep cave which led to the underbelly of the earth. She was there, manifest, standing at the south-west corner of Byres Road by the old G R pillar box on the pavement outside the craft shop. Yet she was not somehow present in her body. Her eyes, unseeing, met nothing and no one over the top of the box. Others, also posting early for Christmas, had simply hooked their hands over Nancy's extended arm, plopped mail in, and hurried on. Hurried on. Hurry on. Hurry on down the road. Hurry on down to the cavernous belly of the underworld. The familiar yet strange place Nancy inhabited knew no cold, no heat, no warmth, no breeze, no wet, dry, nothing but an inky greyness to feel. And that so insubstantial that you had to press your fingertips together constantly in quick rotation to try to feel something, to see if there was anything.

Index, thumb, middle, thumb, ringfinger, thumb, pinkie, thumb, in quick succession to see if there's anything at all except the inky greyness of non-thought, the fudge of falling yet frozen in nothingness.

'Excuse me, hen. I need to get my catalogue order posted – the weans' toys for Christmas, eh?'

'Can you no just budge a wee bit? Okay, pet – disnae matter. I'll just shoogle it in anyway – whoops – there. That's it! . . . Well . . . cheerio, hen . . . and . . . er . . . guid luck eh?'

Thumb, index finger, middle, thumb, ring, thumb, pinkie, thumb, but could she feel the thickness of the envelope between? No, she couldn't if she squeezed her thumb and index together. Only if she squeezed her middle finger and thumb.

The tensing of her finger muscles was the first thing she felt again, then the throbbing aching stiffness. She breathed more perceptibly. *Aaagghhh*. Nancy tried to move her arm and found it painful to do so. A cream mohaired one swung into vision and a fine manicured hand prised the envelope from her frozen, gloved fingers and put it in the box.

'Come into the warm if you can,' a voice soothed in her ear. 'Come away now. Take your time.'

Nancy sat in the craft shop, hunched over on the Lloyd Loom chair, oblivious to the walls covered in Charles Rennie Mackintosh prints and the trail of drifting clove from the pomanders hung from the low ceiling beams.

'Aaghh,' she said over and over again. Mrs Macgregor wasn't sure if it was a sound of pain or relief. Certainly the woman looked rough. Her hair, almost white, was streaked and wet, and the hem was coming down on her coat. One foot tapped restlessly, making an undone strap flap.

It was the only movement the woman made. Mrs Macgregor was afraid she'd collapse as she guided her the eight or so paces from the pillar box to the door of the shop.

Luckily Fiona had rushed to steady the woman at the other side.

'Cup of tea for our customer, please, Fiona.'

Mrs Macgregor noticed the threadbare coat collar, but also the fine chenille scarf, soft and salmony, tucked deeply away at the neck.

'Molly, could you see to the gentlemen?' Molly turned reluctantly back to the two customers near the till, holding fistfuls of shaped candles and posters.

Nancy's foot was still tapping vacantly but not so fast as Fiona brought tea in a pink china cup and saucer. Mrs Macgregor knelt down with it so that she was in the range of vision of the woman.

'A nice sweet tea for you.'

Nancy's lips, clamped but moving restlessly as though chewing a toffee, eased now.

'Aarggh.' She slowly extended a cramped arm, but it cranked down of its own accord before taking the tea.

Mrs Macgregor put the teacup to Nancy's lips. Slowly Nancy tried her arms again. She lifted both hands to the cup and gulped slowly like a child.

'I'm like the tin man,' she said at last. 'I need oiling.'

She stayed in the chair in the same position until past closing time, after Fiona had tallied the takings and had swept off with Molly under a joint umbrella.

Later, in Mrs Macgregor's car, Nancy eased her legs straighter in the calf-level heat. The windscreen wipers swished and sighed. When they reached Nancy's road, Mrs Macgregor fiddled with her keyring.

'You know, I've been like you. I've needed help in the past.'

She looked out over the neat row of terraced houses with their dim lights and straight little gardens. She reached to the back seat for her handbag.

'Here,' she said. 'The name of a very good man', and she slipped a business card and two ten-pound notes into Nancy's still-numb fingers as she leaned to open the passenger door.

The consulting room looked muted and calm, in some ways not dissimilar to the craft shop a week ago, after the customers had gone. Pale-peach carpets and walls, a glass cabinet with books bearing complex titles.

Nancy sat in the chair opposite the man in the grey suit. He had just shaken her hand and now positioned himself with care, it seemed, in his seat, directly in profile to her. His head was slightly bent forward and he crossed one hand over the other.

Nancy seemed to sit there in a way that was as timeless as her spell at the pillar box, except that when she checked her watch afterwards, she knew she had spent fifty minutes in the room.

He had not said much, nor moved, except to flex his fingers once or twice – straight then curled, straight, curled and back to the crossed-hands position.

Before he spoke, Nancy noticed his toe revolved slowly anti-clockwise. He could have been anyone: a bus conductor, a barrister. The receptionist downstairs had told Nancy he was eminent and now worked only privately.

'Please, tell me more about the episode you describe in your letter.'

Nancy felt her fingers working. Thumb, index, thumb, middle, thumb, ring, thumb, pinkie, over and over, both hands together.

'I can't remember,' she began agitatedly, 'but what it *feels* like now is that I was locked away somewhere – probably horizontal, not vertical. Locked away and I was cut, sliced up, like black pudding. And all the bits, all the slices, were tied down with fine string, like fishing line. Thin as thread but strong as gut.

And I wasn't dead, but I wasn't alive either. I could not get any of the bits to touch one another. They weren't in contact with each other except via the thread. I was in a container somewhere deep under the ground. The container was as suffocating as a shoebox and at the same time as roomy as a cave. I could *not* shout out. I tried but I could not.'

The man's eyes lifted to middle distance. He paused at length, then leisurely revolved his chair towards her. His mouth lengthened to a straight line before he spoke.

'You can come and see me again,' he said.

As Nancy closed the door she thought she heard clinking of glass, as though a drink was being poured.

Over the next few days, Nancy thought about the appointment and the man. Although she could not remember what he had said to her, something light and peaceful filled her. She felt like the millstone had at least rolled over.

She began to scan the evening paper for part-time work. She was physically relatively fit. She could attempt something. If she needed to see him again, she would not have Mrs Macgregor's donation to rely on.

A box with bold letters attracted her.

'Artists' models required for day and evening classes. Good rates of pay.' There was a phone number.

Nancy left the flat, closing the brown communal front door and walking past the straight gardens to the telephone box on the corner. She had never owned a phone herself. It would have made her too accessible and vulnerable to the outside world.

When she was connected, she told the tutor she had a lot of recent experience in standing still.

She began the following week. At first one evening only. A trial run, he'd said.

She took to it at once, and was able to sustain difficult poses. The students and the tutor marvelled discreetly amongst themselves at how Nancy could stand leaning on the back of a chair for well over an hour. It was considered a nightmare of a position, involving putting body weight on to the arms, wrists and hands, with a possibility of affecting the circulation.

They marvelled that Nancy breezed through the pose, not seeming to need fortifying cups of tea every thirty minutes, or the ten-minute walk-abouts demanded by other models.

Nancy was offered an immediate short contract until Christmas, with a further one starting next term in January. The tutor thought he could arrange to pay in cash so that Nancy's pension would not be affected.

She had a little trouble with the draught which leaked under the ill-fitting classroom door, affecting her left arthritic shoulder, and riffling the hem of the thin long white skirt she posed in. But the tall student with the stringy hair and the jeans torn at the knee, rushed in with a bulky fan heater, cord spiralling after him like ivy.

For Nancy there was something strange about being still yet aware of time. The large round clock above the dangling anatomical skeleton ticked the seconds noisily. Nancy revelled in the fact that she could count off each. She did not miss one.

She enjoyed hearing each sweep and scratch of the charcoal over thick linen paper.

She basked in the warm pool of arc lights. She was full and exuberant, and part of the world. The world of minutiae. She felt, recklessly, in control.

With her second week's money, she returned to Byres Road, this time in wellingtons. It was really snowing; thick clumps swathing the parked cars in white, and muffling the sound of the moving traffic. Voices carried, clear and ringing: 'Would you look at the state of me? The abominable snowman's no got a look-in.'

She returned to the craft shop, but Mrs Macgregor was out. She bought a wintry Mackintosh print on a card, and Fiona popped it in a flowery bag.

'You're looking better,' she ventured.

'Oh, I am,' said Nancy.

As she stood at the same pillar box, the memories of last month came swirling in slowly, so that soon she didn't know if it were those or the snow in her eyes and mouth that made her breathe in that peculiar shallow jarring way she hadn't experienced since she'd seen Him.

Nancy swallowed and the airmail letter to her penfriend creased as she posted it through the mouth of the box. She kept her fingers on it till the last. Thumb, index, thumb, ring, right through the cycle. But at last she was able to relax enough to rest her head against the domed top, shielding her flooded eyes.

She still had the Christmas card to write to Him, but she couldn't do it here. Snow would encase and numb her bare fingers in two minutes. Glancing round, she saw a café on the other side of the road. Suddenly lit up, its checked table-cloths were caught in a frame of tinsel and fairy lighting. She breathed deeply. Pulling up the rug-like collar of her coat, she walked slowly across.

A Special Case

Moy McCrory

Yellow space, blue locker, yellow space, bed. Yellow space, blue locker, yellow space, bed. Yellow space. Curtains drawn around the. Blue locker, yellow space, bed.

Or try counting the windows.

Snow coming down. Look at the. Snow coming down. Would you look at that snow? When did I last? Terrible winter and people sleeping in the park. Forget how lucky. How lucky.

But I'm not used to this. The noise.

Can only see the sky from this position. Try asking for help in this place. Try asking.

All I wanted was me pillow support fixed up. The one in the next bed has. I slotted it in the frame, punched the pillows, sat up. Felt great. Then bump, bump, bump. I went down a notch at a time. Ring for Sister, the one in the next bed says, She'll show you how to do it. And she just sits there. So I'm wondering if there's something wrong with her legs but I don't say anything. You never know. Then she says, I'll ring the bell, and I say, Don't bother. I'm happy laying flat. I need a sleep. Then they come and draw her curtains.

You know. They ought to have put me in a room of me own. I told them. I said. One of those little ones at the end of the ward. That would do me. They said, Oh, they're for people needing lots of rest. Special Cases.

What the hell am I then?

You're no Special Case.

And I can't sleep, not with all the crashing about that goes on here. They wake you for a cup of tea, six every morning; the one in the next bed told me.

She's gone to theatre now. She says to me, I'll be getting me pre-med in twenty minutes so I'll just say ta ta now, because I'll be talking soft. I looked at her. I was going to say, Do you think there'll be a difference? but I caught myself on. Best to get on with your neighbours. God knows, I could be here for days.

She shouldn't be in with us, but they're packed out so they put her on general.

I should be in the Women's Ward, she goes. I look around. Well, I can't see any men I tell her. No, not that. And she whispers. You know. The Women's Ward. Then she points under her blanket. And I'm thinking I wish they'd get a move on with that pre-med.

I'm having the lot out, she says. I didn't like to ask her, then she said her ovums, so I nodded like I knew.

Funny word. *Ovums*. Ums, ove, ove, ovaltine. It's all technical here.

I should be up there, she goes, and points to the ceiling. Well, she doesn't look that sick, so I tell her, There's plenty of years in you yet, you shouldn't talk like that, and she starts crying. I say, They can do wonders with surgery nowadays. Then a nurse comes over, Who's upset her? and I'm a sitting duck. How did I know she meant the top floor?

How many? I said, Sixteen! They shouldn't build up so high.

Miss Salmon, the nurse said, We are the largest teaching hospital for the entire region.

Was that supposed to calm me down?

The bigger the place, the more chance of them getting you mixed up with someone else. Then the one in the next bed takes off. Wish I'd kept me mouth shut.

Any road, I'm not down to be operated on.

Observation. That's what the nurse said.

They took her just before lunch. She didn't miss much.

She says this morning, I stopped cooking for Him years ago, and he's never noticed.

I didn't know what she was talking about so I said, Does he take himself to the chip shop then? and she looks at me like I've a screw loose.

I get everything from Marks & Sparks, she goes. Meals in a Moment, Birds of Freedom, I've gone through the lot.

Tell you what, I'd be glad of a Meal in a Moment in this place. It takes ages. Out into that room. Plastic seats. And they're supposed to bring you whatever you ticked on the list. Well, I haven't even seen a list, let alone ticked one. You do it a day in advance, so I'm eating what someone ordered before they left. No wonder they went.

At dinner time I'm eating this cheese sauce with like sausage things in, and I say, What the hell do you call this? Give us a look at that menu. And it's saveloys and a portion of something-or-other and I'm on the High Protein, High Energy diet. High blood pressure. And I said, Who's this then? Only there's a name at the top, where you fill your boxes in. And they all go quiet.

Well, when did she go home then? And one of the women, the one with the fallen arches, goes, Well, she was a brave age. You have to expect it.

And I've been sitting there. Eating a dead woman's saveloys.

When they started on their pudding, I just couldn't face it. I looked under the lid; a big dollop of roly-poly, and the custard had gone cold. It's tragic really.

I'm having the one in the next bed's tea. She said she'll not be wanting it, so I had a word with the nurse. Someone else can have the other. I'm getting the egg salad.

Getting the egg. Hard-boiled. Turned navy blue. A ring, isn't it? a blue rim and they go grainy, funny that, but against your teeth they're sort of grainy, sort of. Push them through the egg-slice. Have to do it fast, have to, real fast or they fall, fall apart, go kind of splat. The cutters, little bars, don't go through slowly, have to do it fast. Clean through the boiled egg and it falls in slices, the yolk stays in, but have to be careful, have to get them on to a plate. Arrange the slices, don't let the middle poke out. Maybe some lettuce. Maybe. Same problem with tomatoes. Use a sharp knife. Zap. Keep the middle in. Not the same with the seeds everywhere on the plate, not as nice. Slice them up but keep them entire.

I don't understand. About eggs. You know. Life. Full of mysteries. Why did the chicken cross the road, which came first? But how? I mean, how can you know? When does an egg start becoming a chicken? How does a hen know, how does a hen decide to keep them warm, sit there, trusting something to happen, sit there waiting for the first crack.

The egg must know. It must. I've never understood that. These smart alecs that think they know everything, they can't explain that. How does an egg know it's turning into . . . ? An egg knows, it just does.

I feel sorry for hens. Every day isn't it, laying eggs? Must hurt them. Shitting something that size. Like giving birth. Not that I'd know.

I asked our Alice once. The way she looked at me. You'd have thought I'd said. Something dirty. But some women are driven mad, aren't they? waiting to turn broody.

The one in the next bed said, When I've had this lot out, I'll have flown the coop for good.

That was before she pointed to the ceiling, when she was still speaking to me. Poor sod. Up there, on the Problem Ward where there's no room for her, there's all those women. With their Problems.

I never married, I told her, never gave myself a problem.

But it makes you think. How do you know everything works? How do you? Until you put it to the test. It's too late now. I'm past me sell-by date.

Didn't do our Alice any good. I'm older than her, but you wouldn't know to look at us, not now.

You know. I'll get our Alice to bring me one of the kids'

jigsaws. Anything. Keep me hands busy, stop me mind wandering.

And I've always hated jigsaws. Can't see the point of. Struggle to put a picture together. Pull it all apart again. I'd glue the sides, stick them for ever. Still, something to do. It's that quiet with the one in the next bed gone. Jesus, I must be desperate.

Soft lad Ernest, one Christmas, first after Mam died, buys me five jigsaws. Five of the bloody things. All flowers, laughing children, fluffy puppies. He knows I hate dogs. And our poor Alice, embarrassed for him. He hasn't a clue, she said.

What am I supposed to do with these? I mean, treating me like I was some teenager; and he's laughing, saying he thought it would help to occupy me of an evening, what with being all on me own. Rub it in Mate.

I took them round the thrift shop the next week. Are you sure, Mrs, the woman goes, only they're brand new?

Must be a good time of the year for her, all the bleedin' rubbish people have been given.

No, I say, stick them Right in your Window with one of those Unwanted Present signs. Oh, we haven't got any left. Don't worry, I'll write one out. You're very helpful, she says, I wish everyone was as community-spirited. So that's how I end up doing Tuesdays and Thursdays.

Mostly it's all hats and handbags. You do get some good stuff. There's nice things for kiddies. I put anything I find to one side for Alice's youngest. It can't be easy. And that one was unexpected.

I thought it was the change, Alice says to me. Should have asked me. I could have told her. She tells Ernest they're having a late baby and he looks at his watch. Long as I don't miss the second half he says.

If I see any nice woollies I whip them quick. Hand-knitted, hardly worn, they grow out of things so fast.

What I can't understand are the ones that come in dressed to kill, good leather gloves, court shoes, little diamonds in their ears, and then argue. It's for a good cause, I say. And they stare at you bold as brass. It's frayed at the elbows, they say, as if they've found you out. I mean, it is Sue Ryder, not Jasper Conran.

Had one the other morning, wanted to know if we had it in another colour, and maybe one size bigger. Then the sleeves weren't right. Then the neck was stretched. They'll try anything, some of them. What do they think I'm going to say? Take it off our hands for nothing, you'll be doing us a favour? I said, Oh, I know where there's one just like that. Round the corner in C & A's. And she looks at me. She had good shoes on. I can tell who's needy.

Any road, I'm out in the back putting the kettle on, we'd just had a rush on stocking fillers and had to put the closed sign up. So the other two think they might as well get the till sorted out.

All you have to do is take the ticket off, spike it, then when you add up the coins in the compartments you hope to God they tally after the float. It's not difficult. I can always make them come out even.

Well, someone can't add up. Either that or there's a lot of pinching going on. Who'd be bothered? I mean, if I was going to nick something I'd go to Marks and Spencer's.

So they're struggling on their fingers, I leave them to it. I could kill a cup of tea, I say. Good idea, one of them says.

I call it the back, but it's only a soapstone sink. One tap. And a plug for the kettle, but there's a curtain round it. We take turns to bring in biscuits.

Have to nip over the road to use the lavatories in the park. Public health, close us down if they knew.

Well, one minute I'm waiting by the sink for the kettle, next I'm stretched full-length on the shop floor.

How the bloody hell did I get down here? I say, and of course the old one blushes, likes to pretend she's never heard swearing. You hit your head, one of them goes. You fell and wacked your head on the sink.

Anyway, I try to get up and the shop turns black. So this time I'm frightened.

Run to the greengrocer's and ask to use the phone, the old one's saying, and I think she's talking to me.

I can't bloody run anywhere, use your loaf! Only she doesn't seem to hear me. Then I realise they're not talking to me, they're not even looking at me.

Do you know her phone number? There must be someone. In the book. Next of kin. She lives on her own. Hasn't she got anyone? No. Nobody. What, no friends? Well, I don't know. She must have someone. Where does she live then? It's written in the book. I know that street. Is there anyone we could call? It's a rough street. I think she's got a sister. She must have someone, she's always stuffing clothes into carrier bags.

It's like I'm watching them from the end of a tunnel. Then I think I must be dead. And it would be my luck, I've died and gone to a thrift shop.

Next thing I know I'm being carried by a nice man in a uniform.

I'd always said I had headaches, did I get any sympathy? Started in my late twenties, not that anyone took any notice . . . not me mother, not me family, and I'd been like a mother to them. Well, Mam couldn't cope on her own. Really. You know. I can't remember seeing the inside of any school after that. But it was like I was the sensible one, had no choice, Mam relied on me. Our Alice and Anthony did well at school. He did so well he's got no time to come and see any of us, then Alice gets married, and there's just me and Mam.

When the headaches started? Then.

God, all the questions. They asked me last night. This morning they send me here and there's one waiting with a clipboard wanting to go through it all again. Don't you write anything down, I said. Can't you keep records?

You get used to not making a fuss, you get used to

coping. No point complaining over every twinge. No one to hear you.

I know I was getting headaches then. I couldn't forget. Then Alice had the first baby – you'd have thought I was a teenager the way Mam carried on. All I got was Poor Alice this, Poor Alice that. Alice is tired out. Hardly a word for me. I could have shot myself some days with the headaches. I was blinded. Couldn't walk down stairs. Case I slipped. Might have got some sympathy if I had. Alice wasn't the only one who missed her sleep.

She's been up all night with the baby, Mam would say, as if I'd been awake on purpose.

You can't understand, Mam always said. You've never had kids.

I'd understand if someone would tell me. But no, it's all hush-hush, secret society. I used to go round. Try to help. Then Ernest comes home one afternoon. Didn't know I was in the kitchen.

Thank heavens, he says, We might get a bit of peace, and asks our Alice, oh Big Joke, Why don't we charge her rent, he says, She lives here more than I do.

I wasn't having that. I went into the hall. He pretended he'd meant someone else.

Oh, not you, Peggy, he says, going the colour of one of those crabs in Kenyon's. And Alice, pointing to the door, trying to warn him.

I got me hat and coat.

I'll not stay where I'm not welcome.

You get to be proud, on your own. There's too many waiting to be sorry for you. I don't give them a chance. Every Bloody Christmas it's the same: You can't spend it on your own. Why not? I like me own company.

One year I invited them to dinner but Alice didn't like bringing the kids to Mam's old house. Said the damp affected the little one's chest. Her in her new council house.

You live in this country all your life, and then the likes of Alice's husband, just off the boat, and into a new house.

Me Dad didn't get anything like that when he arrived. They didn't have proper council houses then, I expect, but even if they had, he'd have been the last to know.

But I was born here, I'm as English as the next one. I only went to Ireland once, on holiday, and that soft cow down the road said, Are you going home at last? No I'm not, I told her. This is me home, this is where I live and you'd better get used to it.

I've no chance of getting something better. Not married so bang go me chances.

Now if I'd had kids, I'd have a proper Christmas. I used to hate it, I don't mind it so much now. It's easier with Mam out of the way. But on Christmas morning, there'd be the three of us. Christ, Anthony was a miserable thing even then, and Alice was always ill. Every year, bang on, wake up Christmas morning shivering. But the three of us were always hoping. We never learned. Just for once, I'd think, this year'll be different. Mam was always angry, because . . . a difficult time, because we were kids, and we wanted the same as every other kid. And we got . . . anything cheap and nasty was what we got. Never got anything you wanted. Something small, didn't have to cost the earth, but something you'd like, something she'd spent time thinking about . . . but she never thought. One year, our Alice crying. Couldn't help herself. All she'd wanted was a fountain pen. A bloody . . . Couldn't even manage that. Bloody eau-de-Cologne. Smells like cat's piss. And four bars of fancy soap. Keep them under your bed, I told her, Give them back to her next year. Could have bought two pens for the price. Thoughtless. That's what hurt. We'd creep to bed glad it was over. Can't remember what it was like when Dad was alive. No better. She just got more . . . thoughtless. We never learned. Always disappointed. We just kept on hoping, every year, till we were too old.

If I ever have kids of me own, I said to Alice, I'll do things differently. Well, I didn't and she did.

I love watching her kids open their presents though. See

their faces. Especially the little one. Alice always protests. Peggy, she says, You're spoiling her, Peggy she says, You can't afford to buy for all of them.

Look, I told her, Let them have something worth having, poor little sods. I've no one else to spend me savings on. I am their aunt.

Last year. Nearly caused a riot. The Doll.

Ernest said he'd have to give me half. I wouldn't touch his money.

I don't have to feed and clothe them all year round. I said, I can indulge them once in a blue moon. I can manage the grand gesture.

Manage the grand gesture, you should have seen his face when I came out with that one. He says, I thought it was Alice went to grammar school. And there's our Alice weeping. Let me spoil them, I say, after all the spoiling we never got as kids. And our Alice is in floods at this. Oh Peggy, she says, wasn't it awful? I try to be cheerful, It wasn't that bad.

I'd like to spend Christmas on me own, really, but they won't hear of it. I'd open a tin of Campbells, listen to the radio, sod the TV. All the rows over what to watch.

We're not having that woman in my house, that's Ernest for you. Big Man and he goes and pulls the plug so no one gets the Queen's speech by accident. I don't mind her myself. She's got such nice teeth.

One Christmas, me mother starts, Life's dealt me a cruel hand. Ten o'clock, breakfast things still on the table and she's at it. I can't stand a day of this. We get to Alice's early. I'm making them all coffee. Mam's asking for more, It's nice that, she says. I've slipped her a Mickey Finn.

She slept all afternoon, only woke up once to cry and be helped up the stairs. I didn't say anything. Do you think there's something wrong with me mother? No Alice, she's just tired. She's old. Then Ernest discovers the gin bottle. Jesus Christ, he says, that was full this morning.

Mind you, I've enjoyed the odd Christmas morning since Alice had kids. Christmas is for kids, isn't it? I like being an aunt. I'm their godmother too. Responsible for their moral welfare. I'll make a better job of it than she did for us. We were just left. It was me that sent the other two to school. It paid off though. There's our Anthony, done so well he's no spare time.

Sometimes though, it might have been different, if I'd just gone another way, if I'd stayed at school, if I hadn't been born first.

I never went anywhere, had very few chances, to meet anyone decent. I did meet someone, once. I didn't know it was to be the only chance. Years ago. A feller from the paint factory.

When I was working in the tobacconist's. In town. He used to come for cigarettes and he'd talk. But he was on the rough side. Always wore dungarees, well he was on his way to work. Don't go to the paint works in a suit.

One evening I was locking up the shop. Dreadful cough he had and I turned round, knowing it was His Nibs. He'd been waiting for me. Asked if he could walk me to the bus station. It's a free country, I said.

He didn't look clean. It was the paint. Straight from work, what could he do? Terrible job. He said the fumes got right inside your lungs. I'd always hear him before I'd see him.

I've never smoked. I think it looks dreadful, women with cigarettes. It's different for men, and there's cigars. They give a man class. I always loved the smell of those. The way they sat in the wooden boxes, plump, tanned fingers with silver rings.

Sometimes a real gent would come in and buy two or three. Put them away inside their jackets or in their briefcases.

One old chap used to have this silver case for his. He came in every month and bought eight Monte Cristo number threes, or was it twos? Can't remember. But one end tapered. Those and the Bolivars were the most expensive in the shop. I had to keep the display case locked.

They roll them in leaves, it's all done by hand out in Cuba. I read about it. The *National Geographic* in the library. It was freezing and the radiators were blasting out. There was an old boy asleep by the encylopedias. No one wanted to move him in case he was dead. You know how it it. I'd been waiting for the old one to turn up with the keys to the thrift shop and she never did. Something to do with her daughter-in-law. Any road after that we got our own sets. But there I was standing about on the step. Frozen. So I thought to hell with this. I've had enough.

There was a queue outside the library and suddenly they're all inside. Like the Salvation Army. So I walked in to stop from keeling over with the wind. I just flicked through some magazines and there was this picture. Funny seeing it. All these laughing Cuban women standing in a row. So I read about how they do it, roll cigars like the ones I'd had to lock up. Like the ones the old chap always bought.

He always wore a buttonhole, was a dapper little figure. Must have been good-looking when he was younger. He was polite too. Not like the apprentices. Cheeky little sods. Two looseys, Missus they'd shout from the street. And every morning, before the factory bus, the others would run in, Twenty Woodies! Every day, always twenty Woodies.

I used to look at their teeth. You get to be an expert on smokers' teeth, working in a place like that. Some had mouthfuls of orange ones, loose and gapped like tombstones. They came in smiling with mouths like death. It would put you off.

I've never smoked. Looks awful when you see women doing it. Mind you, Princess Margaret smokes and she wears a headscarf, all the Royals do when they're at the races.

At school, the odd times I was there, they used to say we weren't fishwives. If they saw a girl in a headscarf they'd take it from her. Common. Not fishwives. Poor Pauline Kenyon. Her dad was the wetfishman. Her mother really was . . . Can't remember if she ever wore a headscarf. Well, now no one bothers, women get up to all sorts and no one seems to care. They sit in pubs drinking big, dark pints of stout and who passes comment?

Martini, that's me, with a little cherry and a slice of lemon. Dainty.

Any road, those that smoke, just keep doing it. The feller from the paint works, his lungs were wrecked from the chemicals, I don't suppose it made much difference how many he smoked.

Do you want to meet me one night, after work? he says.

Under the big clock. It was turned half past eight. I'd missed the bus and had to run all the way from the exhange building, right round the back, where the old hospital used to be.

I got all of a fluster and a tizz. Funny how excited I was. Didn't want him thinking I was too keen.

I almost didn't recognise him only he was standing right under the clock. He didn't see me. I didn't like to shout.

Blue suit. Too big. Must have borrowed it. Hung off him. Looked wrong. The shoulders, too wide.

And the shoes.

I hate men in brown shoes. Now they wear all sorts, but then it was black or your working boots. I should have known we weren't suited then.

He'd greased his hair down. It was a yellow colour but that night it looked darker. He'd made an effort. His face was mottled. Looked as if he'd had to scrub to get the paint off.

I was twenty-three. Our Alice was going out with Ernest, and she was only a teenager, but I was twenty-three and anyone I'd been at school with was married with two already in a pram.

I'd borrowed her lipstick. I felt funny. Wiped it off on the back of me hand. Had to fiddle for the mirror in me bag. Check it wasn't all over me face. Look a sight. I'd washed me hair. I had good hair. Thick. Wore it in a roll, with a big wave at the front.

You know. I think you grew old faster then, I really do. I look at photographs and I wonder. It was the clothes. The ones of me mother! In her thirties. Younger than I am now, and she's an old woman.

Twenty-three and I'd never been out with anyone before. I knew I was a freak. I wanted to turn and run.

I didn't know what to say to him. And he was awkward.

What would you like to do? he said, and I didn't have a clue, I just stood there.

He suggested going for tea. It was far too late, I knew it was closed but we went and stood outside anyway.

Embarrassed. I suppose he didn't like to suggest a pub, not the first time, I might have got the wrong idea.

We walked back to the Rialto but we'd missed the start and they wouldn't let us go in late. I told him, I prefer the theatre myself, loud enough so the snooty thing in the box office would hear.

We sat in a café next to the picture house. That's the Bingo Hall now. The café was pulled down, ten, more, years ago.

Do you read? I asked him and he said, No.

Sometimes, after I'd locked up the Bolivars and shut for the day, I'd drop in there for a cup of tea, just sit for ten minutes. I stopped running for buses a long time ago. I wasn't in a hurry to get home. I'd go there and sit. Remember him. Imagine him walking in, older. He'd smile: Aren't you? he'd say. Do you remember that time when we . . . ? Then he'd say something like. You were right, there's another world in books. I'm a professor at a university now, thanks to that night.

He'd no education. Well, neither have I. I missed out. But I've always tried to improve myself. I'm a great reader, I can lose myself in a book.

We sat in the café and he said, No, I'm not much of a reader. I wasn't any good at school. I couldn't wait to get out, to start working.

He ordered me a plate of sandwiches. I told him, they have evening classes, you could go, learn foreign languages, but he laughed. What good's a foreign language to me? And I couldn't explain.

The waitress told us they were closing in half an hour. Slammed the plate on to the table. That wasn't necessary.

And the bread wasn't fresh but there was no point making a fuss. He asked me something, and I started choking. My eyes were streaming. He reached over to clap me on the back only I got up quickly and he missed. He gave me his handkerchief and I fled to the ladies. I half expected him to be gone when I came out.

There were mirrors behind the counter, and I could see him reflected all along the wall. He didn't see me. He was staring out of the window. There was something about his face, when he was quiet, not trying so hard.

Any road, he didn't see me till I was right on top of him and he stood up, wanting to be a gentleman I expect.

The seats were rigid, fixed to the floor. He must have forgotten. He fell against the table, and all the cups went flying. I had hot tea all down my good skirt. Here, take my handkerchief he said. Only I already had it.

I didn't see him much after. Couple of times maybe. He'd come in to buy cigarettes. He used to look at the floor. Then he stopped coming in. I expect he gave up smoking. That's one thing I did for him.

They came along earlier. Next Of Kin? Why? Am I dying then? No, you're not, that fat nurse says. Not my fault I can't oblige you dear, I'm nearly saying. And I can't stop thinking about the dead woman, the one whose saveloys I ate.

Didn't she have a family? No. No one.

Didn't have a visitor either, according to this lot. Been widowed for years. Didn't she have kids? and they all go, No.

Terrible dying alone like that, and then, the one with the fallen arches says, Well, she wasn't alone, was she? She was on the ward. She died publicly, with us. Before you were admitted. And they all nod. Like they've got some knowledge I'll never have, you know, before I was on the ward, and they're all some club or something, and I say, What bed? Oh, don't tell me. And that one says, Stop making a fuss, they change the sheets and everything, and the other one says,

Stop winding her up. You're not in it. They wheeled that bed out. Yours was empty for a couple of days.

Do you mean there's one bed less, I ask, and she says, That's about it. They just opened up the gaps between.

Yellow space, blue locker, yellow space.

Give us all a bit more room, she says. Nice that, isn't it? Only I'm not so sure, what with her next to me not able to get on to the right ward and all.

Or I could count the chairs.

They're all weeping and wailing here. I'd forgotten. Four days to Christmas. Look at that snow. No, three days, four when I hit me head, wasn't it? We had the pre-Christmas rush. The old one was bringing mince pies in the next day. Slug of brandy in the coffee. Very festive. I'd put red and green clothes in the window. You're very artistic, that one had said. Not my usual day, but I'd gone in on the off-chance. They were surprised to see me. Beyond the call of duty. Why not? Looking forward to the New Year, mad rush then. Get back in the swing.

Bit of a lull, the holiday. And they all want to be home for it. Then the nurse comes round asking all sorts of questions like: What kind of a place do I live in? You're a single lady, she says. Well? So do you have family close by? Do you share your house, you know, take in lodgers, have a friend? What sort of a bloody question is that? It's just we need to find out if you're social priority. Living on your own and having these dizzy spells. What dizzy spells? I say, and she looks at the name on her file and then goes and checks with the notes on the bed. That's right, she says, dizzy spells. You mean the headaches, I say. Yes, she goes, And forgetting things. What things? I say and she smiles. I've walked right into it.

Any road, I won't mind. I can have a rest. Our Alice will have to come to me. They do a special Christmas dinner too, and there's a social fund for those who have no friends or relatives so they'll have a little something to open on Christmas Day.

I said, I know all about the needy, working in the thrift shop. And they said, Oh, do you, that's nice.

Well, I reckon I can help, I can pass out the dinners. Keep me mind occupied. I'll be more use here, won't I? helping those less privileged than myself. That's what Christmas is about really, isn't it? About charity.

I can't wait to see our Alice's face when I tell her I'm going to be in over Christmas. It's all right, I'll say, You don't have to spoil your Christmas. Don't bring the kids in. Well, maybe Boxing Day. That'll be nice. Maybe they could open some of their presents round the bed. Glad I do things early, I've already taken mine round. Not everyone's as prepared as I am. They're in a blind panic some of them.

They won't let you have kids visiting, will they, not unless they're your own. Well, they're as good as. I'll see about that!

You get these lulls before visiting hour. The ward suddenly goes silent. We each lie here and think. They brought the one next to me back, half an hour ago. She hasn't woken up yet. When she does, she'll be a different woman. You come in here and let them cut you away. Not me. Cut away your past. Set you loose. Set you free. What did she say, daft cow? Fly the coop. That was it. Not me. I've never gone in for that . . .

It's good now I've figured out how to do the curtains. I could be alone, miles away from this. They're not bad, when you've got your curtains drawn they don't disturb you.

Then everyone meets up for tea. We all complain. Love to really.

Every so often one of the nurses pokes a head in to see if I'm okay and I pretend I'm asleep. I don't much feel like talking. That's the way I am. I prefer to keep myself to myself.

Or I could count the flowers on that curtain.

Debbie and Julie

Doris Lessing

The fat girl in the sky-blue coat again took herself to the mirror. She could not keep away from it. Why did the others not comment on her scarlet cheeks, just like when she got measles, and the way her hair was stuck down with sweat? But they didn't notice her; she thought they did not see her. This was because of Debbie, who protected her, so they got nothing out of noticing her.

She knew it was cold outside, for she had opened a window to check. Inside this flat it was, she believed, warm, but the heating in the block was erratic, particularly in bad weather, and then the electric fires were brought out and Debbie swore and complained and said she was going to move. But Julie knew Debbie would not move. She could not; she had fought for this flat to be hers, and people (men) from everywhere – 'from all over the world', as Julie would proudly say to herself – knew Debbie was here. And besides, Julie was going to need to think of Debbie here, when she herself got home; remember the bright rackety place where people came and went, some of them frightening, but none threatening her, Julie, because Debbie looked after her.

She was so wet she was afraid she would start squelching. What if the wet came through the coat? Back she went to the bathroom and took off the coat. The dress – Debbie's, like the once-smart coat – was now orange instead of yellow, because it was soaked. Julie knew there would be a lot of water at some point, because the paperback Debbie had bought her said so, but she didn't know if she was simply sweating. In the book everything was so tidy and regular, and she had checked the stages she must expect a dozen times. But now she stood surrounded by jars of bath salts and lotions on the shelf that went all around the bathroom, her feet wide apart on a fluffy rug like a terrier's coat, and felt cold water springing from her forehead, hot water running down her legs. She seemed to have pains everywhere, but could not match what she felt with the book.

On went the blue coat again. It was luckily still loose on her, for Debbie was a big girl, and she was small. Back she went to the long mirror in Debbie's room, and what she saw on her face, a look of distracted pain, made her decide it was time to leave. She longed for Debbie, who might after all just turn up. She could not bear to go without seeing her . . . *she had promised*! But she had to, now, at once, and she wrote on a piece of paper she had kept ready just in case, 'I am going now. Thanks for everything. Thank you, thank you, thank you. All my love, Julie.' Then her home address. She stuck this letter in a sober white envelope into the frame of Debbie's mirror and went into the living room, where a lot of people were lolling about watching the TV. No, not really a lot, four people crammed the little room. No one even looked at her. Then the man she was afraid of, and who had tried to 'get' her, took in the fact that she stood there, enormous and smiling foolishly in her blue coat, and gave her the look she always got from him, which said he didn't know why Debbie bothered with her but didn't care. He was a sharp, clever man, handsome she supposed, in a flashy Arab way. He was from Lebanon, and she must make allowances because there was a war there. Sitting beside him on the sofa was the girl who took the drugs around for him. She was smart and clever, like him, but blonde and shiny, and she looked like a model for cheap clothes. A model was what she said she was, but Julie knew she wasn't. And there were two girls Julie had never seen before, and she supposed they were innocents, as she had been. They looked all giggly and anxious to please, and they were waiting. For Debbie?

Julie went quietly through the room to the landing outside

and stood watching for the lift. She checked her carrier bag, ready for a month now, stuffed under her bed. In it was a torch, pieces of string wrapped in a piece of plastic, two pairs of knickers, a cardigan, a thick towel with an old blouse of Debbie's cut open to lie flat inside it and be soft and satiny, and some sanitary pads. The pads were Debbie's. She bled a lot each month. The lift came but Julie had gone back into the flat, full of trouble and worry. She felt ill-prepared, she did not have enough of something, but what could it be? The way she felt told her nothing, except that what was going to happen would be uncontrollable, and until today she had felt in control, and even confident. From shelves in the bathroom she took, almost at random, some guest towels and stuffed them into the carrier. She told herself she was stealing from Debbie, but knew Debbie wouldn't mind. She never did, would say only, 'Just take it, love, if you want it.' Then she might laugh and say, 'Take what you want and *don't* pay for it!' Which was her motto in life, she claimed on every possible occasion. Julie knew better. Debbie could say this as much as she liked, but what she, Julie, had learned from Debbie was, simply, this: what things cost, the value of everything, and of people, of what you did for them, and what they did for you. When she had first come into this flat, brought by Debbie, who had seen her standing like a dummy on the platform at Waterloo at midnight on that first evening she arrived by herself in London, she had been as green as . . . those girls next door, waiting, but not knowing what for. She had been innocent and silly, and what that all boiled down to was that she hadn't known the price of anything. She hadn't known what had to be paid. This was what she had learned from Debbie, even though Debbie had never allowed her to pay for anything, ever.

From the moment she had been seen on the platform five months ago on a muggy, drizzly August evening, she had been learning how ignorant she was. For one thing, it was not only Debbie who had seen her; a lot of other people on the lookout in various parts of the station would have moved in on her like sharks if Debbie hadn't got to her first. Some of these people were baddies and some were goodies, but the kind ones would have sent her straight home.

For the second time she went through the living room and no one looked at her. The Lebanese was smiling and talking in an elder-brotherly way to the new girls. Well, they had better watch out for themselves.

For the second time she waited for the lift. She seemed quite wrenched with pain. Was it worse? Yes, it was.

In the bitter black street that shone with lights from the lamps and the speeding cars she hauled herself on to a bus. Three stops, and by the time she reached where she wanted, she knew she had cut it too fine. She got off in a sleet shower under a street lamp and saw her blue coat turning dark with wet. Now she was far from being too hot, she was ready to shiver and shake, but could not decide if this was panic. Everything she had planned had seemed so easy, one thing after another, but she had not foreseen that she would stand at a bus stop, afraid to leave the light there, not knowing what the sensations were that wrenched her body. Was she hot? Cold? Nauseous? Hungry? A good thing the weather was so bad, no one was about. She walked boldly through the sleet and turned into a dark and narrow alley where she hurried, because it smelled bad and scared her, then out into a yard full of builders' rubbish and rusty skips. There was a derelict shed at one end. This shed was where she was going, where she had been only three days before to make sure it was still there, had not been pulled down, and that she could get in the door. But now something she had not foreseen. A large dog stood in the door, a great black threatening beast, and it was growling. She could see the gleam of its teeth and eyes. But she knew she had to get into the shed, and quickly. Again water poured hotly down her legs. Her head was swimming. Hot knives carved her back. She found a half-brick and flung it at the wall near the dog, who disappeared into the shed growling. This was awful . . . Julie went into the shed, shut the door behind her, with difficulty because it dragged on broken hinges, and switched on the torch. The dog stood against a wall looking at her, but now she could see it would not hurt her. Its tail was sweeping about in the dirt, and it was so thin she could see its ribs under the dirty black shabby fur. Its eyes were bright and frantic. It wanted her to be good to it. She said, 'It's all right, it's only me', and went to the corner of the shed away from the dog, where she had spread a folded blanket. The blanket was there, but the dog had been lying on it. She turned the blanket so the clean part inside was on the top. Now, having reached her refuge, she didn't know what to do. She took off her soaking knickers. She put the carrier bag close to the blanket. Afraid someone might see the gleam of light, she switched off the torch, first making sure she knew where it was. She could hear the dog breathing, and the flap-flap of its tail. It was lying down, not far from her. She could smell the wet doggy smell, and she was grateful for that, pleased the dog was there. Now she was in no doubt she had got here just in time, because her whole body was hot and fierce with pain, and she wanted to cry out, but knew she must not. She was groaning, though, and she heard herself: 'Debbie, Debbie, Debbie . . .' All those months Debbie had said, 'Don't worry about anything, when the time comes I'll see everything's all right.' But Debbie had gone off with the new man to Paris, saying she would be back in a week, but had rung from New York to say, 'How are you, honey? I'll be back at the weekend.' That was three weeks ago. The 'honey' had told Julie this man was different from the others, not only because he was an American; Debbie had never called her anything but Julie, wouldn't have dreamed of changing her behaviour for any man, but this 'honey' had not been for Julie, but for the man who was listening. 'I don't blame her,' Julie was muttering now. 'She always said she wanted just one man, not Tom and Dick and Harry.' But while Julie was making herself think, I don't blame her, she was groaning, 'Oh, Debbie, Debbie, why did you leave me?'

Debbie had left her to cope on her own, after providing everything from shelter and food and visits to a doctor, to the clothes and the bright-blue coat that had hidden her so well no one had known. Debbie and she joked how little people noticed about other people. 'You'd better watch your diet,' the Lebanese had said. 'Don't you let her' – meaning Debbie – 'stuff you with food all the time.'

Julie was on all-fours on the blanket, her head between her arms, her fists clenched tight, and she was crying. The pain was awful, but that wasn't the worst of it. She felt so alone, so lonely. It occurred to her that having her bottom up in the air was probably not the right thing. She squatted, her back against a cold brick wall, and went on sweating and moaning. She could hear the dog whining, in sympathy, she thought. Water, or was it blood, poured out. She was afraid to switch on the torch to see. She felt the dog sniff at her face and neck, but it went off again. She could see absolutely nothing, it was so dark. Then she felt a rush, as if her insides were pouring out, and she thought, Why didn't the book say there would be all this water all the time? Then she thought, But that's the baby, and put her hand down and under her on the blanket was a wet slippery lump. She felt for the torch and switched it on. The baby was greyish and bloody and its mouth was opening and shutting. Now she was in a panic. Before, she had decided she must wait before cutting the cord, because the paperback said there was no hurry, but she was desperate to get the cord cut, in case the baby died. She found where the cord came out of the baby, a thick twisted rope of flesh, full of life, hot and pulsing in her hand. She found the scissors. She found the string. She cut the birth cord with the scissors, and trembled with fear. Blood everywhere, and the dog had come close and was sitting so near she could touch it. Its eyes were saying, Please, please . . . It was gulping and licking its lips, because of all the blood, when it was so hungry.

'You wait a bit,' she said to the poor dog. Now she tied the cord up with the string that had boiled a long time in the saucepan. She was worrying because she was getting something wrong, but couldn't remember what it was. As for boiling the string, what sense did that make, when you

saw the filth in this shed? Tramps had used it. The dog . . .
other dogs too, probably. For all she knew, other girls had
given birth in it. Most sheds were garden sheds, and full
of plants in pots, and locked up. She knew, because she
had checked so many. Not many places where a girl could
give birth to a baby in peace and quiet – or a stray dog
find a dry place out of the rain . . . She was getting giggly
and silly, she could feel herself losing control. Meanwhile,
the baby was lying in a pool of bloody water and was
mouthing and pulling its face about, and she ought to be
doing something. Surely it ought to be crying? It was so
slippery. The paperback didn't say anything about the baby
being greasy and wet and so slippery she would be afraid to
lift it. She pulled out the bundle of towel from the carrier and
laid it flat, with the soft pink satin of Debbie's blouse smooth
on top. She used both hands to pick the baby up round its
middle and felt it squirm, probably because her hands were
so cold. Its wriggling strength, its warmth, the life she could
feel beating there, astonished and pleased her. Unexpectedly
she was full of pleasure and pride. The baby's perfectly all
right, she thought, looking in the torchlight at hands, feet
. . . what else should she look for? Oh, yes, it was a girl.
Was it deformed? The baby had an enormous cunt, a long
wrinkled slit. Was that normal? Why didn't the book say?

She folded the baby firmly into the towel, with the bottom
of the towel well tucked in over its feet, and only its face
showing. Then she picked it up. It began to roar in short
angry spasms. And now the panic began again. She had not
thought the baby would cry so loudly . . . someone would
come . . . what should she do . . . but she couldn't leave the
shed because there was a thing called the afterbirth. As she
thought this, there was another wet rush, all down her legs,
and out plopped a mass of something that looked like liver
with the end of the thick red cord coming out of it.

And now she knew what to do. She raised herself from the
squatting position, clutching the baby with one arm and using
the other hand to push herself up from the floor. She stood

shakily by the bloody mess and moved away a few paces
with the baby held high up and close against her. At once the
dog crawled forward, giving her a desperate look that said,
Don't get in my way. It ate up the afterbirth in quick gulps.
It hopefully licked the bloody blanket, and briefly lifted its
muzzle to look at her, wagging its long dirty tail. Then it went
back to its place and sat with its back to the wall, watching.
Meanwhile the baby let out short angry cries and kicked hard
in its cocoon of towel. Julie thought, Should I just leave the
baby here and run for it? No, the dog . . . But as she thought
this, the baby stopped and lay quietly looking at her. Well,
she wasn't going to look back, she wasn't going to love it.

She had to leave here, and she was a swamp of blood, water,
God only knew what.

She took a cautious look. Blood trickled down her legs.
And she had actually believed a tampon or two would be
enough! She laid the baby down on a clean place on the
blanket, keeping an eye on the dog. Its eyes gleamed in the
torchlight. She put on a pair of clean knickers and packed in
sanitary towels. She tried to tie the guest towels around her
waist to make an extra pad, but they were too stiff. Now
she picked up the baby, which was just like a papoose and
looking around with its blurry little eyes. She took up the
carrier bag and then the torch. She said to the dog, 'Poor
dog, I'm sorry', and went out, making sure the door was
open for the dog. She switched off the torch, though the
ground was rough and had bricks and bits of wood lying
about. She could just see: there were lights in windows high
up across the street. The sleet still blew down. She was already
shivering. And the baby only had the towel around it . . .
She put the bundle of baby under the flap of the now loose
coat and went quickly across the uneven ground to the alley,
and then through the bad-smelling place and then along the
pavement to a telephone box she had made sure would be
conveniently close when she was looking for the shed or
somewhere safe. There was no one near the telephone box,
no one anywhere around. She put the baby down on the

floor and walked towards the brilliant lights of the pub at the corner. She did not look back. The pub was crammed and hot and noisy. Now what she was afraid of was that she might smell so strongly of blood someone would notice. She could hardly make her way to the toilet. There she removed her knickers with the pads of sanitary towels, which were already soaked. She used one of the guest towels to wash herself down. She went on soaking the towel in hot water and wringing it out, then wiping herself, watching how the blood at once began trickling on to the clean white skin of her inner thighs. But she could not stay there for ever, washing. She rubbed the same towel, wrung out in hot water, over her sticky head. She combed her hair flat. Well, it wouldn't stay flat for long: being naturally curly it would spring back into its own shape soon. Debbie said it was sweet, like a little girl. She filled her knickers with new pads, put the bloody pads into the container, and went out into the pub. Now there was music from the jukebox, pounding away, and the beat went straight through her, vibrating and making her feel sick. She wanted badly to get away from the music, but she bought a shandy, reaching over the shoulders of men arguing about football to get it. Unremarked, she went to stand near a small window that overlooked the telephone box. She could see the bundle, a small pathetic thing, like folded newspapers or a dropped jersey, on the floor of the box. She had first found the shed, then looked for the telephone box, and then hoped there would be a window somewhere close by, and there was.

She stood by the window for only five minutes or so. Then she saw a young man and a girl go into the telephone box. Through window glass streaked again with sleet, she saw the girl pick up the bundle from the floor, while the young man telephoned. She ought to leave . . . she ought not to stand here . . . but she stayed, watching, while the noise of the pub beat around her. The ambulance came in no time. Two ambulance men. The girl came out of the telephone box with the bundle, and the young man was behind her. The ambulance men took the bundle, first one, then the other, then handed it back to the girl, who got into the ambulance. The young man stood on the pavement, and the girl inside waved to him, and he got in to go with them. So the baby was safe. It was done. She had done it. As she went out into the sleety rain she saw the ambulance lights vanish, and her heart plunged into loss and became empty and bitter, in the way she had been determined would not happen. 'Debbie,' she whispered, the tears running. 'Where are you, Debbie?' Not necessarily New York. Or even the States. Canada . . . Mexico . . . the Costa Brava . . . South America . . . The people coming and going in Debbie's flat were always off somewhere, or just back. Rio . . . San Francisco, you name it. And Debbie had said to her. 'One day it will be your turn.' But now it was Debbie's turn. Why should she ever come back? She wanted to have 'just one regular customer'. Once she had said, by mistake, 'just one man'. Julie had heard this, but did not comment. Debbie could be as hard and as jokey as she liked, but she couldn't fool Julie, who knew she was the only person who really understood Debbie.

Now Julie was walking to the Underground, as fast as she could. Her legs were shaky, but she felt all right. All she wanted was to get home. It had been impossible to go home, or even think too much about home where her father (she was sure) would simply throw her out. But now it was only a question of a few stops on the Underground, and then the train. At the most, an hour and a half.

The Underground train was full of people. They had had a meal after work, or been in a pub. Like Julie! She kept looking at all those faces and thinking, What would you say if you knew? At Waterloo she sat on a bench near an old man with a drinker's face, a tramp. She gave him a pound, but she was thinking of the dog. She did not have to wait long for a train. It was not full. Surely she ought to be tired, or sick or something? Most of all she was hungry. A great plate of steak and eggs, that was what she needed. And Debbie there too, eating opposite her.

A plump fresh-faced girl in a damp sky-blue coat sat upright among the other home-goers, holding a carrier bag that had on it, written red on black, SUSIE'S STYLES. Her eyes shone. Her young fresh fair hair curled all over her head. She vibrated with confidence, with secrets.

At the station she had to decide between a bus and walking home. Not the bus; on it there'd almost certainly be someone she knew, and perhaps even from her school. She didn't want to be looked at yet. The sleet was now a chilly blowy rain, with the sting of ice in it, but it wasn't bad, more of an occasional sharp pattering coming into her face and invigorating her. But she was going to arrive home all wet and pathetic, not at all as she had planned.

When she turned into her street, lights showed behind the curtains in all the windows. No one was out. What was she going to do about that coat, wet through, and, worse, hanging on her? Her mother would notice all that space under the coat and wonder. Three doors from home she glanced around to make sure no one was watching, and stripped off the coat in one fast movement and dropped it into a dustbin. Even in this half-dark, lit with dull gleams from a window, she could see blood-stains on the lining. And her dress? The yellow dress was limp and grubby, but the cardigan came down low and hid most of it. This was going to be the dangerous part, all right, and only luck would get her through it. She ran up the steps and rang the bell, smiling, while she clutched the carrier bag so it could hide her front, which was still squashy and fat where the baby had been.

Heavy steps. Her father. The door opened slowly while he fumbled at locks, and she kept the smile going, and her heart beat, and then he stood in front of her, large and black with the light behind him, so that her heart went small and weak . . . but then he turned so she could see his face and she thought. That can't be him, that can't be my *father* – for he had shrunk and become grey and ordinary, and . . . *what on earth had she been afraid of?* She could just hear what Debbie would say about him! Why, he was nothing at all. He called out in a sharp barking voice, 'Anne, Anne, she's here.' He was a man waiting for his wife to take command, crying as he went stumbling down the hall. Julie's mother came fast towards her. She was already crying, and that meant she could not see anything much. She put her arms around Julie and sobbed and said, 'Oh, Julie, Julie, why didn't you . . . ? But come in, why, you're soaked.' And she pushed and pulled Julie towards, and then into the living room, where the old man (which is how Julie was seeing him with her new eyes) sat bowed in his chair, tears running down his face.

'She's all right, Len,' said Anne, Julie's mother. She let go of her daughter and sat upright in her chair, knees together, feet together, dabbing her cheeks under her eyes, and stared at Len with a look that said, There, I told you so.

'Get her a cup of tea, Anne,' said Len. And then, to Julie, but without looking at her, looking at his wife in a heavy awful way that told Julie how full of calamity had been their discussions about her, 'Sit down, we aren't going to eat you.'

Julie sat on the edge of a chair, but gingerly, because it hurt. It was as if she had been anaesthetised by urgency, but now she was safe, pains and soreness could make themselves felt. She watched her parents weep, their bitter faces full of loss. She saw how they sat, each in a chair well apart from the other, not comforting each other, or holding her, or wanting to hold each other, or to hold her.

'Oh, Julie,' said her mother, 'oh, *Julie*.'

'Mum, can I have a sandwich?'

'Of course you can. We've had our supper. I'll just . . .'

Julie smiled, she could not help it, and it was a sour little smile. She knew that what had been on those plates was exactly calculated, not a pea or a bit of potato left over. The next proper meal (lunch, tomorrow) would already be on a plate ready to cook, with a plastic film over it, in the fridge. Her mother went off to the kitchen, to work out how to feed Julie, and now Julie was alone with her father, and that wasn't good.

'You mustn't think we are going to ask you awkward

questions,' said her father, still not looking at her, and Julie knew that her mother had said, 'We mustn't ask her any awkward questions. We must wait for her to tell us.'

You bloody well ought to ask some questions, Julie was thinking, noting that already the raucous angry irritation her parents always made her feel was back, and strong. And, at the moment, dangerous.

But they had expected her to come back, then? For she had been making things easier for herself by saying, They won't care I'm not there! They probably won't even notice! Now she could see how much they had been grieving for her. How was she going to get herself out of here up to the bathroom? If she could just have a bath! At this point her mother came back with a cup of tea. Julie took it, drank it down at once, though it was too hot, and handed the cup back. She saw her mother had realised she meant it: she needed to eat, was hungry, could drink six cups of tea one after another. 'Would you mind if I had a bath, Mum? I won't take a minute. I fell and the street was all slippery. It was sleeting.'

She had already got herself to the door, clutching the carrier in front of her.

'You didn't hurt yourself?' enquired her father.

'No, I only slipped, I got all muddy.'

'You run along and have a bath, girl,' said her mother. 'It'll give me time to boil an egg for sandwiches.'

Julie ran upstairs. Quick, quick, she mustn't make a big thing of this bath, mustn't stay in it. Her bedroom was just so, all pretty and pink, and her big panda sat on her pillow. She flung off her clothes and waves of a nasty sour smell came up at her. She stuffed them all into the carrier and grabbed from the cupboard her pink-flowered dressing gown. What would Debbie have to say about that? she wondered, and wanted to laugh, thinking of Debbie here, sprawling on her bed with the panda. She found childish pyjamas stuffed into the back of a drawer. What was she going to do for padding? Her knickers showed patches of blood and that meant the pads hadn't been enough. She found some old panties and went into the bathroom with them. The bath filled quickly and there were waves of steam. Careful, she didn't want to faint, and her head was light. She got in and submerged her head. Quick, quick . . . She soaped and rubbed, getting rid of the birth, the dirty shed, the damp dog smell, the blood, all that blood. It was still welling gently out of her, not much but enough to make her careful when she dried herself on the fluffy pink towels her mother changed three times a week. She put on her knickers and packed them with old panties. On went the pyjamas, the pink dressing gown. She combed her hair.

There. It was all gone. Her breasts, she knew from the book, would have milk, but she would put on a tight bra and fill it with cotton wool. She would manage. In this house, her home, they did not see each other naked. Her mother hadn't come in for years when she was having a bath, and she always knocked on the bedroom door. In Debbie's flat people ran about naked or half-dressed and Debbie might answer the door in her satin camiknickers, those great breasts of hers lolling about. Debbie often came in when Julie was in the bath to sit on the loo and chat . . . Tears filled Julie's eyes. Oh, no, she certainly must not cry.

She stuffed the bag with the bloody pads and her dirty clothes in it under her bed, well to the back. She would get rid of it all very early in the morning before her parents woke, which they would, at seven o'clock.

She went down the stairs, a good little girl washed and brushed, ready for the night.

In the living room her parents were silent and apart in their two well-separated chairs. They had been crying again. Her father was relieved at what he saw when he cautiously took a look at her (as if it had been too painful to see her before), and he said, 'It's good to have you home, Julie.' His voice broke.

Her mother said, 'I've made you some nice sandwiches.'

Four thin slices of white bread had been made into two sandwiches and cut diagonally across, the yellow of the egg prettily showing, with sprigs of parsley disposed here and there. Hunger sprang in Julie like a tiger, and she ate ravenously, watching her mother's pitying, embarrassed face. Why, she thinks I've been short of food! Well, that's a good thing, it'll put her off the scent.

Her mother went off to make more food. Would she boil another egg, perhaps?

'Anything'll do, Mum. Jam . . . I'd love some jam on some toast.'

She had finished the sandwiches and drunk down the tea long before her mother had returned with a tray, half a loaf of bread, butter, strawberry jam, more tea.

'I don't like to think of you going without food,' she said.

'But I didn't, not really,' said Julie, remembering all the feasts she had had with Debbie, the pizzas that arrived all hours of the day and the night from almost next door, the Kentucky chicken, the special steak feeds when Debbie got hungry, which was often. In the little kitchen was a bowl from Morocco kept piled with fruit. 'You must get enough vitamins,' Debbie kept saying, and brought in more grapes, more apples and pears, let alone fruit Julie had never heard of, like pomegranates and pawpaws, which Debbie had learned to like on one of her trips somewhere.

'We aren't going to pester you with questions,' said her mother.

'I've been with a girl. Her name is Debbie. She was good to me. I've been all right,' said Julie, looking at her mother, and then at her father. *There, don't ask any more questions.*

'A girl?' said her father heavily. He still kept his eyes away from Julie, because when he looked at her the tears started up again.

'Well, I haven't been with a boyfriend,' said Julie, and could not stop herself laughing at this ridiculous idea.

They were all laughing with relief, with disbelief . . . they think I've been off with a boy! What were they imagining? Julie contemplated the incident in the school cloakroom with Billy Jayson that so improbably had led to the scene in the shed with the dog. She had joked with Debbie that it would be a virgin birth. 'He hardly got it in,' she had said. 'I didn't think anything had really happened.'

Probably Billy had forgotten all about it. Unless he connected her leaving school and running away from home with that scene in the cloakroom? But why should he? It was four months after they had tussled and shoved and giggled, she saying, 'No no,' and he saying, 'Oh come on, then.'

'Are you going back to school?' asked her mother carefully. 'The officer came round last week and said you still could. There are two terms left. And you've always been a good girl before this.'

'Yes, I'll go back,' said Julie. Seven months – she could manage that. She'd be bored, but never mind. And then . . . This was the moment she should say something more, explain, make up some lies, for they both sat staring at her, their faces full of what they had been feeling for the long five months she had been gone. She knew she was treating them badly, refusing to say anything. Well, she would, but not now, she was suddenly absolutely exhausted. Full of hot tea and food, she felt herself letting go, letting herself slide . . . She began to yawn and could not stop. But they did not suggest she should go to bed, and this was because they simply could not believe they wouldn't get anything more from her.

But there was nothing she could say. She looked at her father, that cautious, greyish, elderly man, sitting heavily in his chair. At her mother, who seemed almost girlish as she sat upright there in her pretty pale-blue dress with its nice little collar and the little pearl buttons down the front. Her grey curls were sprightly, and her blue eyes full of wounded and uncomprehending innocence. Julie thought, I wish I could just snuggle up to Mum and she could hold me and I could go to sleep. Surely this must have happened when she was small, but she could not remember it. In this family, they simply did not touch each other.

Full of the clarity of her exhaustion, and because of what

she had learned in the last months, she saw her parents and knew that – they cancelled each other out. Debbie would say there was something wrong with their chemistry. They did not disagree. They never raised their voices, or argued. Each day was a pattern of cups of tea, meals, cups of coffee and biscuits, always at exactly the same times, with bedtime as the goal. They seldom went out. They saw very few people, only each other. It was as if they had switched themselves off.

They had been old when she was born, was that the trouble?

At Debbie's people shouted, kissed, hugged, argued, fought, threatened, wept, and screamed.

There were two bedrooms in that flat. Debbie had given her the little one to herself. She was supposed to make herself scarce when Debbie came in with a man, a new one, but not when Derek was there, Debbie's real boyfriend. Derek joked a lot and ordered Julie about. How about making me a cup of tea, getting me a drink, making me some bacon and eggs, what have you been doing with yourself, why don't you get yourself a new hairdo, a new dress? He liked Julie, though she did not like him much. She knew he was not good enough for Debbie.

Soon Debbie would get rid of him. As she had the man who once owned the flat and took a percentage of what she earned. But Debbie had found out something bad about him, had put the screws on, got the flat for herself, worked for herself. Julie had seen this man just once, and he had given her the creeps. 'My first love,' Debbie joked, and laughed loudly when Julie grimaced. Derek did not give her the creeps, he was just nothing! Ordinary. Boring. But the man Debbie had gone to New York with was a TV producer. He was making a series no one had heard about in England, not good enough to sell here, he said. This man was more like it, but Julie thought Debbie would get rid of him too, when something better came up.

All these thoughts, these judgements, so unlike anything ever said or thought in her own home, went on in Julie's mind quite comfortably, though they wouldn't do for herself. Debbie had to be like this, because of her hard life. This included something bad that Debbie had never talked about, but it was why she had been so good to Julie. Probably, just like Julie, Debbie had stood very late in a railway station, pregnant, her head full of rubbish about how she would get a job, have the baby, bring it up, find a man who would love her and the baby. Or perhaps it had been something else to do with being pregnant and alone. It was not she, Julie, who had earned five months of Debbie's love and protection, it was pregnant Julie, helpless and alone.

Oh, yes, Debbie was fond of her.

Sometimes she spent the night in Debbie's big bed because Debbie could not bear to sleep alone. She got scared, she said. She could not believe that Julie wasn't frightened of the dark. Debbie always crashed straight off to sleep, even when she hadn't been drinking. Then Julie cautiously got up on her elbow and bent over sleeping Debbie, to examine her, try and find out . . . Debbie was a big handsome girl. Her skin was very white, and she had black shiny straight hair, and she made up her lips to be thin and scarlet and curving, just right for the lashing, slashing tongue behind them. When she was asleep her face was smooth and closed, and her lips were ordinary, quite pathetic Julie thought, and there was wear under her eyes. That face showed nothing of why Debbie said to people coming into the flat who might notice Julie the wrong way, 'Lay off, do you hear? Lay off, or I'll . . .' And her scarlet lips and her black eyes were nasty, frightening.

But if Debbie woke in the night, she might turn to Julie and draw her into an embrace that told Julie how little she knew about love, about tenderness. Then Julie lay awake, astounded at the revelations this big hot smooth body made, and went on making, even though Debbie was off to sleep again. She never actually 'did anything'. Julie even waited for 'something' to happen. Nothing ever did. Just once Debbie put her hand down to touch the mound of Julie's stomach, but took it quickly away. Julie lay entangled with Debbie, and they were like two cats that have finished washing each other and gone to sleep, and Julie knew how terribly she had been deprived at home, and how empty and sad her parents were. Suppose she said to her mother now, 'Mum, let me come into your bed tonight, I'm scared, I've missed you . . .' She could just see her mother's embarrassed, timid face. 'But Julie, you're a big girl now.'

Anne and Len slept in twin beds stretched out parallel to each other, the night table between them.

There were tears in Julie's eyes, and she did not know it, but then she did and looked quickly at her mother, then her father, for they must not know she would give anything to cry and cry, and be comforted and held . . . But they weren't looking at her, only at the television. They had switched it on, without her noticing. Now all three of them sat staring at it.

On the screen a woman announcer smiled the special smile that goes with royalty, animals and children, and said, 'At eight o'clock this evening a newly born baby girl was found in a telephone box in Islington. She was warmly wrapped and healthy. She weighed seven pounds and three ounces. The nurses have called her Rosie.' Hot waves of jealousy went through Julie when she saw how the nurse smiled down at the little face seen briefly by Julie in torchlight, and then again through the sleet outside the shed. 'The mother is urged to come forward as she might be in need of urgent medical attention.'

It was the late news.

Surely they were going to guess? But why should they? It was hard enough for her to believe that she could sit here in her pretty little dressing gown smelling of bath powder, when she had given birth by herself in a dirty shed with only a dog for company. Four hours ago, that was all!

'Why don't we have a dog, Mum?' asked Julie, knowing what she was going to hear.

'But they are such a nuisance, Julie. And who's going to take it for walks?'

'I will, Mum.'

'But you'll have finished school in July, and I don't want the bother of a dog, and I'm sure Len doesn't.'

Her father didn't say anything. He leaned forward and turned off the set. The screen went blank.

'I often wonder what Jessie thinks,' he remarked, 'when she sees something like this on the telly, I mean.'

'Oh, leave it, Len,' said Anne warningly.

Julie did not really hear this, but then she did; her ears sprang to life, and she knew something extraordinary was about to happen.

'That's why we were so worried about you,' said Julie's father, heavy, grief-ridden, reproachful. 'It's easy enough to happen, how were we to know you weren't –'

'Len, we agreed we wouldn't ever –'

'What about Auntie Jessie?' asked Julie, trying to take it in. A silence. 'Well, what about her, Dad? You can't just leave it like that.'

'Len,' said Anne wildly.

'Your Auntie Jessie got herself into the family way,' said her father, determined to say it, ignoring his wife's face, her distress. His face was saying, Why should she be spared when she's given us such a bad time? 'She wasn't much older than you are now.' At last he was looking straight at Julie, full of reproach, and his eyes dripped tears all down his face and on to his tie. 'It can happen easy enough, can't it?'

'You mean . . . but what happened to the baby? Was it born?'

'Your cousin Freda,' said Len, still bitter and obstinate, his accusing eyes on his daughter.

'You mean, Freda is . . . you mean. Auntie Jessie's mum and dad didn't mind?'

'They minded, all right,' said Anne. 'I remember all that well enough. They wanted the baby adopted, but Jessie stuck it out and had it, and in the end they came around. I still think they were right and Jessie was wrong. She was only seventeen. She never would say who the father was. She was stuck at home with the baby when she should have been out enjoying herself and learning things. She got married when she was a baby herself.'

By now Julie was more or less herself again, though she felt as if she'd been on a roller-coaster. Above all, what she was thinking was, I've got to get it all out of them now, because I know them, they'll clam up and never talk of it again.

'Didn't Uncle Bob mind?' she asked.

'Not so that he wouldn't marry her, he married her, didn't he, and she had a love child he had to take on,' said her father, full of anger and accusations.

'A love child,' said Julie derisively, unable to stop herself. But her parents didn't notice. 'That's what they call it, I believe,' said her father, all heavy and sarcastic. 'Well, that's what can happen, Julie, and you've always been such a sensible girl and that made it worse.' And now, unbelievably, this father of hers, whom she had so feared she ran away from home, sat sobbing, covering his face with his hands.

Her mother was weeping, her eyes bright, her cheeks red.

In a moment Julie would be bawling too.

'I'm going to bed,' she said, getting up. 'Oh, I'm sorry Mum, I'm sorry Dad, I'm sorry . . .'

'It's all right, Julie,' said her mother.

Julie went out of the room and up the stairs and into her room, walking carefully now, because she was so sore. And she felt numbed and confused, because of Aunt Jessica and her cousin Freda. Why, she, Julie, could have . . . she could be sitting here now, with her baby Rosie, they wouldn't have thrown her out.

She didn't know what to think, or to feel . . . She felt . . . she wanted . . . 'Oh, Debbie,' she cried, but silently, tucked into her little bed, her arms around the panda. 'Oh, Debbie, what am I to do?'

She thought, In July, when I've finished school, I am going back, I'm going to run away, I'll go to London and get a job, and I can have my baby. For a few minutes she persuaded herself it was not the silly little girl who had run away who said this, but the Debbie-taught girl who knew what things cost. Then she said to herself, Stop it, stop it, you know better.

She thought of Aunt Jessie's house. She had always enjoyed that house. It occurred to her now that Debbie's place and Aunt Jessie's had a lot in common – noisy, disturbing, exciting. Which was why her parents did not much like going there. But here, a baby here, Rosie with her long wrinkled cunt here . . . Julie was laughing her raucous, derisive laugh, but it was unhappy because she had understood that Rosie her daughter could not come here, because she, Julie, could not stand it.

I'll take Rosie to Debbie's in London, said Julie, in a final futile attempt.

But Debbie had taken in pregnant Julie. *That was what had been paid.*

If Julie brought baby Rosie here, then she would have to stay here. Until she got married. Like Auntie Jessie. Julie thought of Uncle Bob. Now she realised she had always seen him as Auntie Jessie's shadow, not up to much. She had wondered why Auntie Jessie married him. Now she knew.

I've got to get out of here, she thought, I've got to. In July I'll leave. I'll have my O levels. I can get them easily. I'll work hard and get my five O levels. I'll go to London. I know how things are, now. Look, I've lived in Debbie's flat, and I didn't let myself get hurt by them. I was clever, no one knew I was pregnant, only Debbie. I had Rosie by myself in that shed with only a dog to help me, and then I put Rosie in a safe place and now she's all right, and I've come home, and I've managed it all so well they never even guessed. I'm all right.

With her arms around the panda Julie thought, I can do anything I want to do, I've proved that.

And she drifted off to sleep.

Contributors' Notes

Joan Anim-Addo was born in Grenada and educated there up to the age of thirteen. Since then she has lived and worked in London and Lusaka. She has taught all her adult life and now lectures part time in higher education.

Petronella Breinburg hails from Surinam (also known as the Dutch West Indies) in South America where she has been a school teacher. Though Petronella is best known for her 'Sean' books which pioneered picture books with Black children playing a positive role, she has published a long list of children's stories, plays and academic papers. Petronella Breinburg is at present a senior lecturer in the department of English at Goldsmith's College.

Glyn Brown, ex-sign writer and motorbike messenger, is a freelance journalist whose work has appeared in *The Guardian*, *The Times Literary Supplement*, *City Limits*, *Blitz*, *Melody Maker* and *i-D*, amongst others. She won the 1990 *Time Out* Short Story competition, her story, 'Flight', was published in the anthology *The Word Party* (The Centre for Performing Arts) and she is presently tussling happily with her first novel. She lives in North London, sustained by her two cats, her typewriter and a charming man. She has been known to enjoy the odd bit of weight-training.

Alison Campbell writes mainly short stories and children's books. She has recently completed counselling training and is currently co-editing a fictional anthology of stories around the theme of the ages and stages of women.

Mary Ciechanowska was born in Yorkshire but has lived all her adult life in London, most of it with her husband and two daughters. She has also been writing for most of it, working with her husband on books, papers, features about war-time Polish history while, in her head, doing writing of a different sort. This recently got its chance of life and paper when more time came her way and she is working on a collection of short stories and setting out towards a novel. She studied sociology at LSE but has found out more about human society – its best, its worst – from teaching in London comprehensive schools.

Fiona Cooper is the author of five novels: *Rotary Spokes* (Black Swan, 1990), *Heartbreak on the High Sierra* (Virago, 1989), *Not The Swiss Family Robinson* (Virago, 1991), *Jay Loves Lucy* (Serpent's Tail, 1991) and *The Empress of the Seven Oceans* (Black Swan, 1992). She has contributed to numerous short story collections and written articles and features for the gay press as well as collaborating on film, TV and radio scripts. She is currently working on a book of short stories for Serpent's Tail. She lives with dozens of tropical fish, two daft dogs and her beautiful 'significant other' five minutes from the sea in Northumberland.

Eleanor Dare was born beside the River Thames at London Bridge. Now she lives in Camberwell. Quite a traveller, really.

Julia Darling lives in Newcastle-upon-Tyne with her two daughters, Scarlet and Florrie. She works as a freelance writer and has had a number of plays produced by companies in Newcastle and Sheffield. Previous publications include a collection of poems, *Small Beauties*, published by Newcastle City Council. She writes for, and performs with, The Poetry

Virgins, a female troupe of actors and writers, who tour the North East extensively, although never get south of Sunderland. As a poet in her own right, she has performed in Germany and Holland.

Margaret Elphinstone has worked as a writer and a gardener, and has published gardening books as well as poetry and fiction. She is the author of two novels, *The Incomer* (The Women's Press, 1987) and *A Sparrow's Flight* (Polygon), and a collection of short stories, *An Apple from a Tree* (The Women's Press, 1988). She teaches English studies at Strathclyde University, has two daughters, and lives in Edinburgh.

Caroline Hallett lives and works in North London, where she has helped to set up a counselling service for young people. Writing is an interest that persists alongside job, training and family of three small children. She writes short stories and is gradually adding to a number which she hopes to make into a collection. She is co-editor of this anthology.

Susan King was born in Birkenhead in 1952. She left school when she was sixteen but returned to full-time education ten years later to take a degree in Sociology at Salford University. She now lives in North London and divides her time between lecturing and writing. In the last year she has won a number of prizes in literary competitions, including first prize at the 1992 Southampton University Writers' Conference for her short story 'Gastric Measures'. She is currently working on her first novel.

Doris Lessing was born in Kermanshaw, Persia, now Iran. As a child she lived in Rhodesia, now Zimbabwe, on a 2,000 acre farm. She left school at fourteen and has worked as an au pair, a telephone operator and a legal shorthand typist. She was heavily involved in left-wing politics, where she learned a lot about groups, their natures and function, and about power. She moved to England in 1949, where she sold her first novel, *The Grass is Singing*. She is now a major, acclaimed novelist.

Doris Lessing has been married twice and has three children. She lives in London.

Ann Chinn Maud was born in Los Angeles, California in 1931, grew up in Salt Lake City, Utah and now divides her times between Minneapolis, Minnesota and London. She is presently working on a series of autobiographical stories names after popular songs of the period to be collected under the title *Songs My Mother Never Taught Me* as well as a book about the medieval iconography of the dance.

Moy McCrory has written three collections of short stories and more recently a novel, *The Fading Shrine* (Jonathan Cape) as well as numerous pieces in anthologies. Her second collection, *Bleeding Sinners* (Jonathan Cape), came out to critical acclaim and she was awarded an Arts Council bursary. Her first book was a Feminist Book Fortnight Selected Twenty Title, as was her novel. She has had work broadcast on radio and TV.

   She was the creative writing tutor for the University of London's post-graduate media course, and teaches creative writing at numerous venues, including Arvon. She was writer in residence for the Salisbury Festival.

   She has two young children.

Jay Merill was educated at King's College, London. She writes poetic prose and prose-poems, and has written several novels and screenplays. She is currently working on a number of fragments which might be brought together into a whole novel or might persist as isolates.

Carole Morin was born in Glasgow and went to school in New York. After studying at Harvard, she worked briefly as an actress. She was Associate Editor of *Granta* magazine, after which she converted to Catholicism. She now lives in London. She wrote her first novel, *Lampshades* (Secker & Warburg), while suffering from a tubercular toe. *Lampshades* has been described as 'a fictional voyage of total taboo that is exhilarating, clever and utterly new' (*Sunday Times*). The paperback will be published by Minerva in October 1992.

Jenny Palmer was born in Colne, educated at Clitheroe, and read German at Reading University. She has travelled widely and is now settled in Hackney, teaching EAP (English for Academic Purposes) to international students at Goldsmith's and King's Colleges. She has published widely on Third World Issues in *Spare Rib, Outwrite, Everywoman, Tribune, The Socialist* and *Textile Horizons*. She took up fiction writing six years ago and has completed a novel and quite a number of short stories. She is currently working on her second novel arising out of a recent trip to Bolivia. She is a founder member of the collective which put together *The Man Who Loved Presents* and *The Plot Against Mary*, and co-editor of this anthology.

'First Kiss' is an extract from a longer piece entitled *Nowhere Better Than Home*.

Joanna Rosenthall was born and brought up in Leeds. Her family are second generation Jewish immigrants from Lithuania. She currently works as a psychotherapist and writes in what bits of time there are left. Some of her stories have appeared in assorted anthologies and one in *Critical Quarterly*. She lives in North London with her husband and daughter, Esther.

Marijke Woolsey lives in South Tottenham in North London with her husband, two daughters and a female lodger. She always writes from a female perspective, which apparently makes her work uncommercial. An editor described the novel she is working on as 'intelligent women's fiction'. She is hoping an intelligent publisher will want to buy it.

Zhana's previous work includes *Sojourn* (Methuen), an anthology exploring relationships between and among Black women, which she edited and co-authored. She is a performance poet and is currently working on a novel, entitled *The Treasures of Darkness*, and a collection of poetry, entitled *Sisters and Other Goddesses*.

Also of interest:

eds Campbell, Hallett, Palmer and Woolsey

The Man Who Loved Presents

The old woman laughed; cackled from her stomach. 'In one generation? In one universe! Three wise men. You've got to be joking!'

And after that they settled down to the important task of birthing her baby daughter.

The Man Who Loved Presents is the bestselling predecessor to *The Plot Against Mary*, a sparkling, original collection, giving new meaning to the season of goodwill.

A host of top women writers and talented newcomers, bring short stories bursting with fresh perspectives and exciting new insights. From horror to humour, biting satire to the macabre and the fabulous, these tales examine the turbulence of family gatherings, the volatile meetings of generations and the tantalising traumas of excessive eating, drinking, and entertaining.

The Man Who Loved Presents is a powerful antidote to standard seasonal fare, inverting normal perceptions of what the festive period means – a lively and entertaining reappraisal of traditional cheer.

Fiction £6.99
ISBN 0 7043 4289 8